The Rapist

Praise for
The Rapist

"Les Edgerton is the king of hard-edged, bad-ass crime fiction, and *The Rapist* is his most harrowing book yet."
—Scott Phillips, author of *The Ice Harvest*

"Les Edgerton presents an utterly convincing anti-hero. The abnormal psychology is pitch-perfect. *The Rapist* ranks right up there with Camus' *The Stranger* and Simenon's *Dirty Snow.* An instant modern classic."
—Allan Guthrie, author of *Slammer*

"Edgerton's brilliant archaeological dig into the motivations of a rapist is an unflinching look at the darker recesses of the human psyche."
—Richard Godwin, author of *Apostle Rising*

"Les Edgerton's *The Rapist* is for those brave enough to acknowledge the ugly reality produced by our illusions. . . . It poses hard questions and makes you look hard for answers. This is great, challenging literature."
—Lee Thompson, author of *When We Join Jesus in Hell*

"Take a Nabokovian narrator trying to convince the reader of his innocence and filter it through 'An Occurrence at Owl Creek Bridge' and you've got *The Rapist*, a raw and frightening journey through the inner psyche of a damaged man."
—Brian Lindenmuth, publisher of *Spinetingler Magazine*

“. . . the breathlessness, nausea, anger, and confusion increase all the way to the end, at which point all I know is that the book is genius.”
—Helen Fitzgerald, author of *Dead Lovely*

“*The Rapist* blends Camus and Jim Thompson in an existential crime novel that is as dark and intoxicating as strong Irish coffee. Les Edgerton pulls us into the corkscrew mind of Truman Ferris Pinter, a twisted man with skewed perception of the world, as his life spirals toward oblivion, like dirty dishwater down a plughole.”
—Paul D Brazill, author of *13 Shots Of Noir*

“Les Edgerton’s book *The Rapist* is Albert Camus’ *The Stranger* retold as if by the lovechild of Edgar Allen Poe and Charles Bukowski. . . . This tale, with its many twists and turns, is definitely not for the faint of heart—but then, the title should have made that clear.”
—Scott Evans, Editor, *Blue Moon Literary and Art Review*

“This intellectual tour-de-force rips open the mind of a delusional psychopath taking the reader on a raw journey that challenges Dante’s Inferno. And the last line of the book is the penultimate example of a sociopath’s naked ego.”
—R.C. Stewart, author of *The Blackness of Darkness*

“*The Rapist* is a challenging novel, not for the squeamish, and definitely not for anyone who dislikes being pulled out of their comfort zone. It quite simply blew me away. Destined to be a classic.”
—Heath Lowrance, author of *The Bastard Hand*

"This is a different voice than we're used to, a different kind of hunger. What's new here is the abandon. This is the kind of work you get from a writer with nothing left to lose, not one with nothing left to prove, and that's the biggest surprise of all."
—David James Keaton, author of *Fish Bites Cop!*

"Les Edgerton proves once again why he is one of the most exciting writers of this generation… [*The Rapist*] is one of the bravest pieces of fiction you are likely to read this year, and also one of the best. This is a novel you'll want to read again and again; an outstanding read!"
—Luca Veste, author of *Liverpool 5*

"[*The Rapist*] is one of those books that each time you read it, you find another kernel of truth, a pearl of wisdom. It has that many facets wrapped in rich layers of dialogue, characterization and setting that pounded with each of the rapist's heartbeat. I was hooked from the first page."
—Wendy Gager, author of *A Case of Infatuation*

"Like Denis Johnson's classic novel-in-stories, *Jesus' Son*, Les Edgerton's *The Rapist* is a dark, risky, disturbing story that grabs the reader in a haunting fashion and holds on tightly. The writing is taut and unsettling. Edgerton is a mighty talent."
—Tony Ardizzone, author of *The Whale Chaser*

"A unique, riveting look into the mind of a very disturbed character. Tough to read, but tougher to put down. Only a writer with Les Edgerton's skill could pull this off."
—Terrence P. McCauley, Author of *Prohibition*

"*The Rapist* is a disturbing look into the twisted mind of a narcissistic psychopath on death row. A vulgar odyssey reminiscent of Nabokov's Lolita, although far more depraved, Les Edgerton has crafted a dark and brilliant story that leaves you as equally unsettled as it does in complete awe."
—Julia Madeleine, author of *No One To Hear You Scream*

"A deathdream swan dive from the existential stratosphere plummeting into the personal hell of a tormented, broken psyche... Les Edgerton melds introspection and visceral, human brutality in this death row narrative from a masterful storyteller, whose dissection of a psychopath will haunt you long after the final page."
—Thomas Pluck, editor of the anthology, *Lost Children Protectors*

"Les Edgerton's masterly *The Rapist* is a deeply disturbing journey into the murky recesses of the mind of psychopathic death row inmate Truman Ferris Pinter.... Sympathy for The Devil, indeed, in this dark vision of a black heart that is both astoundingly honest and ultimately terrifying."
—Lesley Ann Sharrock, author of *7th Magpie*

"Against all odds, master wordsmith Edgerton has created the most mesmerizing and disturbing narrator since Patricia Highsmith's Tom Ripley, an intense, strange, well-spoken villain whose story and sexual perceptions will frighten many more men than women. *The Rapist* is not who—or what—you think."
—Jack Getze, Fiction Editor, *Spinetingler Magazine*

"I wouldn't say that after you finishing reading *The Rapist* you're going to have a feeling of satisfaction. In fact, I strongly suggest you're going to feel as if you've just walked out of a House of Mirrors. You certainly will be confused, shocked, and puzzled. But *you will* realize that you've just read something amazingly original. Truly, magnificently, original."
—B.R. Stateham, author of *A Taste of Old Revenge*

"In *The Rapist*, author Les Edgerton has penned potentially a career-defining work, challenging societal notions of right and wrong, crime and punishment, religion and philosophy, and wrapping the whole thing up in a taut, breathtaking, utterly absorbing account of narcissism, self-absorption and unchecked ego."
—Allan Leverone, author of *The Lonely Mile*

"A writer who writes a book like *The Rapist* is a writer that holds no fear. That is clear from the outset. It alerts the reader to the fact this will be a challenging read– and it is. A challenge for the reader to trust the writer. Unreservedly. Trust the writer will keep them safe. In Les Edgerton, you are in the safest of hands."
—Ian Ayris, author of *Abide With Me*

"I'm thrilled to have a new author over whom to obsess. It's been a while since I discovered Ted 'Get Carter' Lewis, Elmore Leonard and Thomas Harris. Decades since I saw my first Tarantino. Les Edgerton belongs in that company."
—Mark Ramsden, author of *Dark Magus and the Sacred Whore*

"Years ago, the poet Ezra Pound issued his one and only commandment to all the writers and poets who would follow in his footsteps: 'Make it new.' Since then, many have tried. Most have failed. But Les Edgerton, in *The Rapist*, obeys that commandment to the letter. Les guides you home to port astounded, much wiser than you were—and in complete awe of the ambition and success of this sudden classic."
—A.J. Hayes, noir poet, published in numerous venues

"Les Edgerton's *The Rapist* reads like congress with the Devil himself—elegantly unsettling and with a hell of an after-taste."
—Jedidiah Ayres, author of *Fierce Bitches*

"A brilliantly narrated tapestry of violence, sex, and death in American heartland, *The Rapist* is a must read for all noir aficionados and serious readers of hard-boiled lit. Once again Les Edgerton proves that he is not only a master of the modern noir novel, but a literary stylist capable of delivering a contemporary classic."
—Vincent Zandri, bestselling author of *The Remains*

"Les Edgerton is the real deal, his work consistently unflinching and raw. And his new novel is no exception. Reminiscent of Hubert Selby Jr.'s *The Room*, Edgerton's *The Rapist* takes us deep into the mind of a disturbed man. And while some would label the character a monster, Edgerton is much more interested in finding whatever shred of humanity he can within the darkness. Ambitious and provocative, as every novel should be."
—Johnny Shaw, author of *Dove Season*

“If you were familiar with Les Edgerton’s work—you aren’t anymore. *The Rapist* marks a whole new direction for the noir stalwart. He strips Kafka of genteel niceties and leads us on a searing voyage into the black beating heart of an implacable sociopath. *The Rapist* will leave you jittery for days and wondering what damaged human depths there remain for Edgerton to plumb.”
—Court Merrigan, author of *Moondog Over the Delta*

“There aren’t many modern books like this, I’m pretty sure. Though it may not always be a fun ride, there’s an element of satisfaction for the reader who takes this on in undertaking such a perilous journey. I left *The Rapist* battered, bruised and exhausted—what more can one say about a book than that?”
—Nigel Bird, author of *Mr Suit*

“I just finished *The Rapist* and . . . um . . . wow . . . just . . . I mean, holy . . . what a voice. What a . . . I mean, it’s so . . . wow. Damn. Seriously.”
—Eric Beetner, author of *The Devil Doesn’t Want Me*

A NEW PULP PRESS BOOK

First Printing, March 2013

ISBN-13: 978-0-9855786-2-6

ISBN-10: 0-9855786-2-9

Printed in the United States of America

Visit us on the web at www.newpulppress.com

For Mary, Britney,
Sienna, and Mike

The Rapist

Les Edgerton

Foreword

I was sitting in the Trident Bookstore Café in Boulder, Colorado in the summer of 2010 when I had the experience of reading Les Edgerton's novel, *The Rapist*. I mention the exact time and location because just as time plays an incredibly important part in his story, the book itself gave to me one of those reading experiences which crystallizes you on the spot, freezing you in your chair and in time and space as you are transported. I'll mention that reading the pages of *The Rapist* does not produce a static feeling—it is more like getting hurled through a plate glass window—but the actual experience was similar to that of being frozen in time, in Mr. Edgerton's time, in his transcendent art.

There is an exchange in Hemingway's *The Green Hills of Africa* between the Hemingway narrator, also a writer, and a German kudu hunter. They are sitting around the campfire discussing literature. The German asks the Hemingway character, "Do you think your writing is worth doing as an end in itself?" What follows is a sort of metaphysical homage, a prayer almost, of what is possible when fiction works:

"The kind of writing that can be done. How far prose can be carried if anyone is serious enough and has luck. There is a *fourth and fifth dimension* that can be gotten."

"You believe it?" asks the German.

"I know it."

"And if a writer can get this?"

"Then nothing else matters. It is more important than anything he can do. The chances are, of course, that he will fail. But there is a chance that he succeeds."

"But that is poetry you are talking about?"

"No. It is much more difficult than poetry. It is a prose that has never been written. But it can be written without tricks and without cheating. With nothing that will go bad afterwards."

Perhaps Hemingway was correct that this fourth dimension has never been written, but as a lover of fiction that takes risks and pushes against the current boundaries of how far literature can go, I've had the feeling of being in contact with stories that bravely attempt to discover this land of the fourth dimension in fiction. With each book I could tell you where and when I was when I read it. It was this way with *The Rapist*.

As I sat down to read *The Rapist* on that summer afternoon, my expectations were that I would be reading another excellent, dark, sparely-rendered work of noir fiction by a writer who we had first published in the crime fiction magazine, *Murdaland*. I had read many of Edgerton's novels and even a hard-punching memoir, and always had the feeling that Les held a special place in American crime fiction. Because of his background as a convicted felon who lived in the actual world of criminals, his novels and stories always possessed that veracity like that of Edward Bunker that many modern crime writers lack. Unlike Bunker, however, Edgerton's prose had the discipline and ear of a unique and singular artist. To me, and I can never escape this, his voice was a hard poetry of the streets that avoided pretension yet delivered literature all the same, reminiscent of Charles Bukowski. In short, I always believed that Les Edgerton should be and would be a memorable and lasting voice in American fiction. But as I started this novel, *The Rapist*, I was a little bit taken aback. The narrator, Truman Ferris Pinter, is a pretentious, conceited sociopath, unlike any of Edgerton's hardened, street-wise thugs that had come before. And while the book starts out with a gangbang and a rape, it somehow moves at a much slower pace than Edgerton's other novels. Truman Ferris Pinter launches into invectives about the institutions of marriage and religion, and has historical asides about how Native American mothers would insert their babies' penises into their mouths to quiet them when enemies were lurking. Truman reads Andrew Marvel and Aeschylus, rapes without mercy, and weighs with an inner rage upon all the injustice, stupidity, and foolishness of American society. And so I read, realizing this was no Edgerton "noir," that this was something more, a dark, literary experiment, and I waited for that moment, hoped Edgerton could pull it off and take me beyond…and then Truman begins to fly. The final 2/3s of the novel warp and shrink and conflate with a pink-eyed madness, and I realized at the end that Edgerton had pulled something off: something thought-provoking and incredible.

When I put the book the down, I felt like I had when I was 21 years old and had just finished Hubert Selby's novel *Last Exit to Brooklyn.* I was riveted, fractured, and throttled. Reading the novel had been almost completely a physical experience…and then I realized the author, as Hemingway says in *Green Hills of Africa,* had not cheated but had brought me back home without tricks, but with raw honesty. The end result was a sort of exhausted exhilaration, the feeling of having been taken beyond the normal reading experience.

I think *The Rapist* is Les Edgerton's tour de force among his many other accomplished and wonderful noir novels. The tendency might be to try to classify and intellectualize this book. With its existential themes and the sometimes nihilistic tone of Truman, it might be tempting to liken this book to Camus' *The Stranger* or some Sartre play. I would like to caution against this. *The Rapist,* with its propulsive force, its indignant fury, its rage against institutionalization, its seething violence seen in both a detailed gangbang and rape, is, perversely but inherently, an American work of fiction: brash and petulant like a cowboy kicking his way through the double doors to the saloon; self-confident in its unlikable individuality like a boastful Charlie Manson; and shot through with a pure black-hearted anger and indignant rage as of the kind you can only get in the United States of America, the Land of Opportunity, where democracy is espoused, but the Nietzschean Will to Power and Ragnar's Might Makes Right rule the day. This book is his poem, his testament, his art boiled down to its elemental genius. Edgerton's vision, while it seethes, ultimately dissolves rage and hatred in its pages and, as it lifts you up... way up above Earth, emerges with something better on the other side, something that only literature in its finest moments can provide.

—Cortright McMeel
Thanksgiving Day 2012

The past, present, and future exist at
the same time, as is proved by our dreams.

—John Donne, recurring theme.

Chapter One: The Present

Let me tell you who occupies this prison cell. Perfidious, his name is Perfidity. His name is Liar, Blasphemer, Defiler of Truth, Black-Tongued. He lies down with all members of the congregation equally, tells them each in turn they are his beloved, while he is already attending to the next assignation in his relentless rendezvous with the consumption of souls.

He will inhale you, devour you, eat the pulp of your soul and spit out the husk. Behind his eyes lies nothing save the fevered light of unholy candles. He is black magic without redemption, without even the nethermost quality that could be termed human, or rather, he is not that at all; he is *all* that is estimated human, the sum total of those values that achieve the color that is the presence of all colors: black. He lacks a center—each of you is his center—and he has sucked the marrow dry of each of those he has visited. Beware of the son of Moloch that paces to and fro in that barred room.

This unholy creature is none other than the author of this narrative, Truman Ferris Pinter, which is the name my parents bestowed upon me, to which the State has added the further qualifier, Prisoner #49028. And these preceding words are but the insidious defamations of the man that unfairly prosecuted me and caused me to be sentenced to die by my own choice of execution, either hanging or firing squad?—hours from now? The summary of the time left me escapes my attention. It is not true that the condemned man savors and counts each eroding second that is left to him.

Perhaps after reading this account you will come to a different conclusion about who I am. Perhaps not…

I will tell you my story in chronological order, for I feel, even at this great distance in time and place, that you are much younger than I and no doubt raised on an insipid diet of television. Your attention span would be a single digit near zero and your comprehension of anything penned less than that, so I will keep it simple and direct. And in order. So as not to confuse you.

I actually saw her the night before the rape.

I was wheeling my bicycle past the town tavern. I had no profession then, never have, before or since, as my father was a prudent man, investing heavily into life insurance to the tune of nearly a million dollars, and my mother had the grace to expire during my twentieth year, leaving the bulk of the estate to me, her only progeny. I suppose I do have a profession of sorts: husbanding my inheritance and making it grow, but that is a job that requires little of my time. Mostly, it involves choosing a manager wisely and then standing aside and letting him go about his job. I do, or did, various things to occupy my waking hours, much reading, some writing, a little angling, taking a beer at the local tavern and so on. A gentleman's life is what I aspire to, by temperament and situation, and it suits me well. I enjoy an intelligent conversation, and while such is a rare commodity in these parts, from time to time the odd professor or well-read graduate loses his way and ends up at our tavern, and we share a beer. I can turn a phrase or two when the audience is capable, and I know a thing or two of Homer and other savants, and my reticence only extends to yokels and sophists, of which sadly, the world appears filled to overflowing at present. Should Charon flow today, the ferryman would require three shifts, multiple crews, and a six-span bridge besides.

Keeping on, in the night in question, I was on my way home from my weekly marketing and elected to pass by the tavern instead of entering. I am by no means a habitué, setting foot inside, at best, thrice monthly, so it was not unusual to continue past Joe's Tavern (ingenious name!) as I did that evening.

It was just past nine, and as our orbits around the sun are exact, I am sure you know, as it pertains to this latitude, at this time in the summer solstice, in July, you would realize at once that a full moon adorned the heavens and provided enough illumination to read a standard newspaper held at arm's length. So it was as I pedaled my two-wheeler past crude and raucous laughter, almost certainly directed at one of Joe's two buxom barmaids, and, if tavern events were holding to custom, probably in response to some raw remark referring to anatomy, specifically breasts. I grimaced at the sound, disgust washing over me. I had attempted more than one conversation with these waitresses, whose names were Jo and Beth (I sense unrewarded optimism on their mothers' part in affixing such gentle names on the fruit of their wombs, stubborn, misplaced hope that they would turn out as well-bred and docile as Miss Alcott's creations) and had discovered that decorum was not the path to either's heart, each preferring the clumsy advances of what you and I would refer to as "rough trade."

I digress. That is my nature; I admit the fault. A thought flits by here, then there, and I must follow; it is the curse of the nimble mind. All the while that I am pedaling furiously, however, I can see the main road and know that the path I have taken will lead back to it eventually. If you ride with me, trust me; I shall have you back on the wider highway, sooner or later. Is it not on the smaller trails that we sneak up on truth? Such has been my experience. You may get there faster with your blind drive, but will you know how you got there or even why? I think not. The hermit whom the uninitiated would seek, sits not by the side of the road as the poet would have you think, but by the side of the *barely visible path*, hidden behind the milkweeds and goldenrod, and you fool yourself if you think he waits for you; he waits for no man and is hard to find for a reason.

I was past the tavern and entering the small wood that sprawls just past it, situated between the tavern and my own modest house, the same house I was born in and grew up in. Did I mention that? There is a small path, negotiable only by foot or bicycle, that is a shortcut to home. Midway into this copse, which means fifty yards into the wood, I heard voices and laughter. Curiosity aroused, I laid down my bike safely off the path and stole back through the trees to see what goes. I was naturally furtive in my movements, not wishing to disturb what I honestly thought to be unknown persons engaged in innocent and wholesome activity.

I was wrong...oh, how I was wrong! There were several persons, to be sure, but innocent was not the name of their game. They were engaged in the act of sexual intercourse, one by one, three men and a girl. They seemed to be just beginning, the girl still removing clothing and the men standing in a respectful semicircle, watching her.

Propriety suggested that I leave at once, but as I've stated before, I'm human, and I gave in to my venal side, opting to remain where I was secreted and watch, like Fabian. I am ashamed, I admit it, but would you have done otherwise? I think not. There are certain things we are all bound up in together, regardless of class or station, and this is one of them. I think certain weaknesses will always be with us, no matter to what plane we evolve.

I didn't mark the time I stood there, concealed by a dead oak of magnificent girth.

Initially, I wasn't aware of what was happening. It was just three men and a girl. Two of the men I recognized as being regulars at Joe's Tavern—common drunks. The third looked familiar, but I couldn't place him in the dark, not being able to see his features clearly. The woman kept running back and forth from man to man, giggling as she'd peck one on the cheek and then another, her hand flying to her hair after each buss. I could hear her juvenile giggling, and she'd shriek when one reached out to take her by the waist, squirming free to skip up to the next one, breaking away from him as well and on to another; round and round she went. One of the loose women whom I'd also seen at Joe's many times, cadging drinks from fawning men as she flitted from table to table. I couldn't recall her name.

Then they began to encircle her, and she was in the midst of their circle, still giggling but now with a somewhat hysterical sound to her laughter. They all stopped in their tracks to stare when she reached behind her, unhooked the tube top she was wearing, and released her breasts. She tossed the top, and one of the men reached out and plucked it out of the air and brought it to his face and buried his nose in the material. I could hear the sharp intake of one of the men and realized I was holding my own breath.

Her breasts shone with perspiration in the moonlight. I forced a moan back from my own lips and felt my member become turgid and painful against the prison of my trousers.

One of the men approached her and knelt in front of her. He reached up and put his hands on each side of her shorts and tugged them down. She helped him by shimmying her hips, stepped out of them when they hit the ground and lifted them with her foot, flinging them in the face of one of the other men. The men laughed raucously, and she shrieked again and giggled as the man who'd taken her shorts off rose and bent over, kissing and sucking on one of her breasts.

And then they had their carnal pleasure with her. I saw each of the three insert, in turn, his penis into the girl and fuck her, twice each. It was interesting to observe the various lovemaking styles of each, and I was amazed at the difference in the size of each man's organ. One was so small as to be laughable, as indeed the girl did, her hooting causing him to redden and tremble, observable even in the darkness, but her scorn didn't appear to deter him as he thrust into her with short, violent strokes. The time he gave her was as thrifty as his weapon, and the girl only looked mildly disappointed when he withdrew, but not much so, as I'm sure she realized there were better moments to come from the others.

She moaned from time to time, from deep inside her

belly, a low, almost savage and bestial sound that, I confess, aroused me to the precipice, again and again.

At the end, with the last man, she must have been exhausted. She turned over on her belly and, with great effort it seemed, lifted her buttocks, glistening with her moisture, into the air and allowed the last man to enter her from behind.

This seemed to renew her energy and her libido as she began to growl, a sound mindful of a bear or other feral creature, and thrust back at the man. I could plainly see the expression on his face—a mixture of terror and passion—as he desperately tried to keep up with her, but it was plain that she was in control of both him and the situation, and I realized she had been in control all along. Of her. Of the men.

Of me.

To complete this story, after a bit, one of the men produced a bottle of wine or whiskey—it was difficult to tell which at my distance—and they all sat on the grass and talked among themselves in loud voices. The slattern, who I recognized now as Greta Carlisle, at last jumped to her feet, seemingly none the worse for the experience, and began walking back toward Joe's. The others sat there a moment until she disappeared, then stood up, voices lower now than when she'd been there, and two of them went in the direction Greta had gone and the other turned and went though the wood to his left. I could hear him crashing through the underbrush as he made his way to who knows where.

Later, at home as I lay abed and recalled the event, I relieved my sexual pressure yet again.

That was the night before I raped her. You can decide if my action on that day was warranted or justified. Or, if it was even a rape.

...a digression. Some background...

My earlier history is unimportant. I was born without the use of forceps, in the same bed used to conceive me—what mixed images my mother must have had whenever she changed the sheets!—coming from safe darkness and the gently rocking sea of the womb into a hard, brilliant light and white noise, my birth being natural and containing nothing more than mundane trauma. Reared by a loving mother, whose features, quite frankly, escape me even now, as they have for some time. I seem to associate sticky things with her, like clear Karo syrup and the kind of white paste we used to be given in grammar school and would sometimes nibble on, its flavor being a jejune one akin to that of processed bread . I know she lavished mindless physical affection upon me, as I recall in Technicolor and Panavision endless hours of being forced to sit upon her lap as she churned me back and forth in a scratched up brown rocker, a tint mindful of cowpies. I can recall one time in particular when I was being rocked to the point of nausea and thinking I would like to reverse the situation and subject her to endure twenty-four hours nonstop of this cretinous torture, but, being only six at the time of the thought and not physically able to carry out this wish, could only hold it against her for the rest of my life. I am too harsh in my memory, as I am sure she was what those not privy to her rocking fetish would classify as a "good" mother, but she wasn't what I would have shopped for had God placed me in a more rational world, one in which we could chose those who are to tend to us until we are able to manage our own affairs.

About my father; I barely knew him. He was some sort of drummer or something and always away, for which I adored him in his good sense. He died in some sort of accident when I was nine years of age, and the funeral was very lovely. I remember a sense of great enjoyment during the whole affair. I have but fond memories of him and hope that someday we may meet again under circumstances more pleasurable than I find myself in at present. Perhaps on the morrow we shall shake hands, man to man, if we are to believe our zealous Christians and their mawkish folklore as to what transpires after earthly death. As for me, I pretend not to know what lies ahead. I certainly don't have the headstrong surety God's lambs possess.

Perhaps we are all returned to life in the form of mosquitoes, which would certainly explain why there are so many of them. If so, I would hope for a sex change in the next life as I am itching to sting someone.

During my childhood, I kept no journal or diary, nor am I into statistics in any meaningful way, but a quick and rough calculation puts the number of times that I masturbated at some nine thousand times, give or take a few hundred drops of spermatae, between the ages of eight and eighteen, and since that age, although I had slowed down until these past few months, there have been probably at least that many instances again where, alone in my room, I have fondled myself to the point of release.

I can imagine your smile. You think, "If only he had abused himself just the one more time he would not be here today," but you must not think like that. I didn't, and I'm here, and the why or how is not important, only the facts are important, and the fact is I didn't masturbate that day, and as a result I sit here preparing to die. Think of it in this light. If I had spilled my seed upon the ground instead of performing an act against society, to wit, committed a rape, then neither of us would be here and what would you have done with this time? Watched another television show? Read a cheap fiction? Hardly what one would consider uplifting now, is it? So be thankful that there are doers in the world (both yours and mine) and that everyone is not a simpering, passive creature such as you.

The next morning after my witness of the goings-on in the wood, I had all but forgotten the incident except briefly while drinking my first *cafe au lait*, but I dismissed it out of hand at once. Last night was last night and today was today. To suffer the vicissitudes of memory is the desperate and shallow act of lesser men: those unfortunate enough to be burdened with a mind empty of weightier thought. When exercising the function of memory, I had more profitably recalled a sonnet of Andrew Marvell or a scene from Aeschylus, both examples far loftier than grubby, nefarious depravations of some inconsequential peasants as they mucked pathetically about on the primeval floor of the forest dark.

It was at that moment that I made one of those decisions that, as they are endlessly saying, changes the course of your life forever. I was scheduled to receive a haircut that morning but elected to forego the appointment and go fishing instead at the river whose banks wind in lazy esses a quarter of a mile from my abode. I, of course, did the proper thing and phoned Harry the barber (I've always chuckled at his name) and canceled my appointment in sufficient time for him to refill it. It's best to treat others as you would like to be treated, and even though Harry is, of course, merely a tradesman, I give him the benefit of the doubt and count his time valuable, at least to him.

I remember being in a jejune mood that morning as I prepared my fishing tackle. I had decided against live bait, selecting surface plugs to take instead. Angling inevitably puts me into a sanguine mood. I suffer the company of others, but enjoy solitude more, and fishing is the definitive form of that joyous state. I highly recommend it and prescribe it as a palliative for that most intelligent of all conditions, misanthropy, or the specialized subset, misogyny. A fish is an excellent substitute for, say, a wife. The piscatorial species accept instruction with good humor and practice stoicism, two fine qualities never discovered in any but the rarest of the female species. I know that it (fishing) has aided and abetted me in my approach to life on many occasions. The hours I have spent thus employed have been both enjoyable and utile, the activity allowing me to contemplate in peace and achieve a state of utter relaxation at the same time. That is a side of my nature that you doubtless find difficult to comprehend, considering the short time we have been acquainted, but it exists, I assure you.

Angling is the one arena in which I allow myself to become a competitor. It's just you and your wits against the unknown skulking below you in the murky brown depths. There's a mysteriousness there that compels with it a hint of danger and, at the same time, drops a peace over you like a blissful cocoon.

As I say, my mood was elevated as I left the house, my South Bend spinning rod and reel carried like a rifle over my shoulder, tackle box in my fist, a spring in my step, shoulders thrust back to fill clean, pink lungs with fresh, cool oxygen, eyes clear of troubles.

The jaunt to the river bank and my pet fishing spot was uneventful. It was eleven a.m. by the time I reached my destination, and the July sun was already baking the underbrush to a dry crackle beneath my feet. Where I angled was shaded with thick oak and elm trees with their armfuls of dark waxy leaves, and I was quite comfortable. Nestled in my tackle box was a thermos of icy lemonade and ready next to it a full pint bottle of amber Irish whiskey.

I fished without incident for at least two hours. Not even a hesitant nibble, which is the way I prefer my fishing. If you don't catch anything, there is no work to do and the whole activity is play and you can't name another human enterprise that fits that playbill!

Along about one in the afternoon, I had tossed my plug out into the current for only the second or third time (I have my own unique method of fishing with plugs—it doesn't involve retrieving them as is popularly done—this excites fish and makes them angry enough to strike, which means—you guessed it—work) when I made a mistake and a large carp struck. I should have known then that unpleasant things were about to happen; they had already begun with that imbecile carp. In disgust, I reeled the loathsome creature to shore, jerking my rod tip as I did so, but even that ploy failed to dislodge my catch, and I was forced to take hold of his smelly, vile carcass and unhook him, tossing the wriggling, ugly mutant up onto the bank. If he was so stupid as to impale himself on my hook, I wasn't going to be equally absurd and throw him back and give him the opportunity to ruin a future day of fishing. Directly after, my solitude and good humor destroyed, another alien entered my environment as evidenced by the sound of twigs breaking by some clumsy creature approaching from the same path I had traveled earlier, crashing through the milkweeds and jodhpur like some blind mastodon, shattering the pristine solitude that had been mine up until this instant. The resentment that welled up in me was tempered in a trice by the sight of the creature herself as she bounded into view, and the stern reprimand that was on the edge of my lips transmuted to a harmless, "Hello there," as, I'm sure you've guessed it, one Greta Carlisle (curious blend of Teutonic and Celt in a name) emerged, the girl of the amatory adventures of the previous evening, seemingly fully recovered from the dalliance, no muscle aches in the way she moved or visible bruise marks, and smiling like a starving pig in a vat of sour cream.

Piano keys flashed as she opened her mouth, snapping out a chipper, "Hey, pal," between chomps on her chewing gum, and she proceeded to flop down inches from me without so much as a by your leave or may I, please, working her gum as if she were talking to some pimply youth at a roller-skating rink instead of to a gentleman of substance and property, as she should have, properly.

Everything that makes me who I am, if nothing else, makes me a democrat, with a small d, and I therefore refrained from delivering the lecture she deserved on manners, presenting my own by way of instruction.

"Good day, again," I said. "My name is Truman. I'm very pleased to meet you, miss."

On her body were articles of clothing disallowed at most religious gatherings. Covering her breasts (barely) was a tank-top, and it was arranged in such a fashion as to expose fully half of her considerable cleavage; the only way to differentiate it from her own skin was that it was a slightly deeper pink. A breeze ruffled up just then to stiffen her nipples to the size, shape, and color of tater tots, those tasteless morsels they sell in shiny plastic bags and, of course, I noticed, which I assume is the point of donning such apparel in the first place. Seeing that I had witnessed this bodily metamorphosis, she coyly arched her back and smiled.

"They call you 'Old Fuckface', is that it?"

That was cruel. Once or twice, I had overheard the appellation and suspected myself to be the object, but not before now had I proof positive. Many in our village didn't like me; they were all jealous of my wealth and superior intellect. One thing was odd about this exchange. Even as she was insulting me, I was becoming sexually aroused. I answered the slut.

"No, that isn't my name. I have already given you my name. Let me ask you a question. Are you always this rude or am I being given special treatment?"

I continued.

"Furthermore, I did not invite you here and quite frankly much prefer the company of that fish to such as you. You are obviously a nitwit with the morals and brains of a common alley cat."

"Yeah. Old Fuckface. That's what Beth at Joe's calls you. Christ, most everybody I know calls you that. You're a joke, bud. Don't talk to me about breeding and crap like that. I'm just as good as you are. Better. Least my old man wasn't a drunk, and he for sure didn't beat my mom up all the time." She laughed, a horrible sound, like a rabbit caught by a barn owl.

"You alla time pretend to be some kinda big shot what thinks he's smart. I got an uncle who's a Certified Public Accountant, and he can talk rings around you." She hooted again, giving the mice heart attacks for miles around. Her mouth chomped open again. "I saw you last night."

This was unexpected. I should have ordered the slattern away at this point.

"You were standing behind that big ol' tree. You was watchin' me and the guys party, and you was whackin' yer petey."

I couldn't believe my ears. And when she said "petey", wouldn't you know it? It got bigger.

"What kind of trollop uses language like that?" I asked, my voice trembling. "I couldn't help noticing you and the hoodlums you were with, for your information. I happened to be innocently on my way home and you were right in my way."

The horrid tramp laughed. Laughed! "On your way home! We were fifty yards from the path. The same path you always ride your bike on like I've seen you do ten thousand million times! Who you kiddin'?"

"Get away," I said.

It was then she stood up and did an astounding thing. She lifted the tank-top up and over her head, exposing her breasts. She stood before me like that for a moment and then said in a haughty voice, "Well, Old Fuckface, that's it. I was gonna let you kiss 'em and maybe give you a roll in the hay, but not now, buster. I thought maybe you wasn't as creepy as everybody makes out, but you're worse than what anyone says. You're a jack-off and a creep besides. You blew it. You can eat your heart out, bud."

My brain exploded with a white heat. I remember only snatches of what happened next. Tiles in a mosaic rather than a complete picture.

How it happened I don't know. She was rising to her feet and then she wasn't. She was pinned beneath my weight. I drifted somewhere above the both of us, floating, detached. I'm two people. One mind, split. One above and emotionless, the other feeling her body beneath me, her open palms bludgeoning my ears until I want to scream, but it's she who screams.

She scratches, deep furrows in my face. One ear feels nearly severed.

Bastard, bastard, bastard! she screams, over and over. Something unintelligible, guttural.

I work between her knees, forcing them apart. I catch her wrists, stop her blows. I feel myself gaining control. She weakens. Screams again, her loudest scream. It penetrates my brain, gives me new strength. I smile, and she sees my smile, and I see the surrender in her eyes. She continues to fight, but we both know who will win.

Holding her wrist still, I slam her with an elbow. She's stunned. I let go of her wrists, and her arms fall to the ground. She looks at me, but there's no recognition in her eyes. She might have been looking at a movie that she wasn't interested in.

I reach down, hook my fingers in her shorts, begin to pull them down, and then they rip and there's no underwear; she's nude save for her tank-top which is even easier to tear off. I throw it aside and it falls in a small, pink heap.

I have the strength of ten lions, and I am so hard. Harder than last night even. I try to enter her and at first I can't. She moans but her heart isn't in it. I push again and I'm in. I feel the skin on my penis tear, and she moans louder, and I grow even harder. It's not possible to be this hard. I thrust, hard, and I'm in all the way, and she feels like sandpaper, and I know we are both bleeding, but nothing will stop me now.

I bring her up to me, feel her breasts on my chest, and I hear her moaning again…but, no! It isn't her moaning. It's me. I can feel her breathing though. It starts and stops and every few seconds she has a sharp intake of air.

It's my first time, and I understand now what the poets speak of. I know now the poets don't have the words. Pretenders, all.

Her eyes roll back in her head, and her mouth lolls open, and I kiss her but she doesn't kiss back. I don't know if she's conscious or not, but it doesn't matter to my pleasure. I find I don't like kissing at all.

No matter.

And then it begins to build. It builds to where I'm in danger of passing out. The pressure mounts in my groin and in my brain, and I know I’m thrusting like a madman, but it feels as if I’m barely moving. She’s panting in time with my thrusts, and at first I think it’s from her own pleasure, but I see that it’s not. Each time I slam into her she pants as the air is forced out of her. She’s panting just to get air back into her lungs to stay alive, and it’s an involuntary action—I see she’s passed out.

That excites me even more. I’m a blur, slamming my body into hers, over and over, and every nerve ending in my body has become my penis, and way down deep inside I begin a sound I’ve never made before. It’s like water sluicing down a deep river, into a dam, and each wave beats against the concrete of the dam, and I see a crack in the structure and that excites me more, and I slam harder and harder, and then it breaks and the water pours through, slabs of concrete thrown aside from the force as if they were made of Styrofoam, and I’m through and it’s. . .ohohohohohohohohohoooooooooooo. . .one long groaning, moaning, straining sound coming from a part of me that’s never been reached.

And I’m done. Like that. I feel nothing now and if I felt something before it’s vanished.

I’m back in my body. My faculties—as they say—are intact.

And that was how I raped her. I don’t deny it, never have. But, I didn’t kill her. She killed herself. It was an accident, pure and simple. After I withdrew from her putrid body—it was all I could do to force myself to even touch her if the truth be known once I orgasmed—she leaped up, cursing and yelling, and ran down the path, screaming she was going to get her boyfriend to come thrash me and castrate me. That was when she slipped and struck her head on the rock and fell into the water and drowned.

How can that be construed as murder? For that matter, how can what I did be called rape, under the circumstances? Would you not have done the same under those circumstances? The woman was a common whore and not capable of being raped. I was within my rights as anyone with a modicum of sense could see.

Look here—there I was, minding my own business, quietly fishing, and this whore of Babylon comes along and pushes me into a situation that was her own doing, wholly.

I'm an honorable man—I think when they came to my house to question me they thought I'd lie or at least make it difficult for them, but I had nothing to hide. I had committed no crime. If the world had been a just place, they would have buried her with a big red A sewn on her burial shroud.

You think me bitter, perhaps. Nothing could be more distant from the truth.

I have given much thought to this concept society defines as rape and have found it wanting. In no other species on earth does such a concept occur, in either your world or mine. You have seen the birds of the air suspended high above the ground engaged in sexual combat, and it seems clear that the female many times has not been a willing participant. Is the male bird murdered or even censured by his fellow avians? Not at all. It is a normal part of their existence. I have heard from reliable sources of horses cruelly nipping and biting mares to force them to their pleasure and have yet to hear of a stallion punished for this activity. Most times, according to my sources, the mare is forced into the situation and held firmly in position by her owner while the stallion has his way with her.

There is still another way to think of this.

If I, or you for that matter, were to go up to a female in a crowded bus station and rub your elbow up against her elbow, would you be tossed into prison? If you grasped one of the opposite sex's hand and violently shook it, would you be condemned to die? If you were to lean down and pat a small girl's head, would you stand trial as a charged felon? You see then, my point.

What is sexual intercourse but the rubbing together of different parts of the body? We attach so much mystery to something that has no mystery, once seen in the light of reason. What makes fucking different from pinching someone's ear? Oh, says one way in the back, afraid to show his face, it is different because it involves *these,* and he points to his puny member and shriveled testicles. Well, think beyond what your mother has told you and what has been told in kind to millions of simpletons who question nothing and therefore discover no truth, and tell me—for I am simple too, in another, purer way—who decided sexual organs were different and why, from say, your left index finger? The iconoclast says further, seeing his argument weaken, but they are the instruments for procreation and therefore sacred, meant to be used only under holy sanction, which customarily means in wedlock, and that is why taking your pleasure is unlawful and a crime against society. Whoosh! That is a laughable and pitiable argument indeed. Who decrees that the penis, which shoots out semen to fertilize the woman's womb and therefore prolong and propagate the species (which is the only reason for such sanctions), is holier than the fist, which destroys the predator and therefore accomplishes the same objective? Or the fingers that plant the wheat that sustains us? They each serve to protect and prolong the species. For that matter, rape itself is instrumental in propagating the species in that many of these so-called perverse acts result in pregnancy. The rapist should be applauded, not reviled. And there is this: to buy the idea of holy wedlock being the only legal basis for intercourse is to buy the idea of a holy God in the first place and the cornerstone for the whole argument...and where does that leave the atheist or, for that matter, the agnostic? If the act occurred among a society (and there are several) that requires the gift of sex from both genders upon request, is it any less a crime? Or is it a crime at all? It would seem to depend upon the society and its own provincial ideas and therefore not a crime against society as some would have us believe but a crime against a particular group or tribe. In some societies it is considered a crime not to provide sex when demanded. If the concept of rape is a crime before God, does that mean that God will punish those societies that don't hold it as such? It seems to me that there is no such crime as rape except as it exists as an invention of archaic societies.

Try this one. In certain North American Indian tribes, it was at one time, before the English "civilized" them, the custom that if an enemy approached their hiding place and silence was crucial to survival for the mothers to put their infant boys' penises into their mouths and suck on them to keep their babes quiet. Such a logical response to danger would doubtless be dealt with harshly by the keepers of the present society, an insane reaction to an ingenuous and logical act of intelligent survival.

The decision has been made to dispose of me, and I have no interest in vainly contesting their verdict.

I didn't start out to rape her. It doesn't really matter what my intentions were, at least not to the men and women who put me in here; their hearts are stone and not capable of recognizing truth in any guise, but I should like someone to know the truth, even if it is only you. You, at least, by the reading of this text, have shown some faint interest in my case, more so than the idiots who sat on my jury; what was on their minds was rushing home as soon as possible to paint a picture of the "madman" they had sentenced to death to their friends and neighbors, their only opportunity in life of achieving any importance. Reflecting from my own notoriety, I am afraid I disappointed them, never once drooling, nor rolling my eyes, nor crying out for mercy, nor "confessing" to anything so venal, nor, in short, acting out any of the roles they had assigned for me in their shallow minds. There was one instance of flatulence, which I shall describe later, but you shall see my behavior to be circumspect and justified in this instance. If they described anything but a dignified, utterly composed gentleman sitting calmly in the docket, they have lied, as I am certain they did. I proved to be poor copy for their sensationalist minds as I sat with honor and decorum whilst all about me lawyers, reporters, judges, jury, spectators and Philistines babbled like baboons on a banana boat. There! You see that? And she said I wasn't a poet! I will show you even more evidence of my talents.

I started to say that my original intent was not rape. When she jumped up and exposed her breasts and spoke to me in that vile manner, I sprang up behind her as she turned and did the low thing; I slapped her across the face. That is my crime. For a brief moment, I forgot my breeding and sank to her level. For that, I should have been punished, and that is for what I accept my punishment now, not for the insensate charge of rape. I acted not the gentleman, and that is what I am above all else. Of all societies' flawed concepts, the one that remains logical is the one of gentility and the only one I can subscribe to as a thinking man. The concept of character is a dialectical one, of great value if ever there is to be a viable society, and I was, for an instant, guilty to the marrow of not being such a person. On that basis I accept death as a just penalty but not for the other. Not for rape. And not, most assuredly, for murder.

She screamed when I smote her, and I lost control. I detest, no, abhor with a white-hot abhorrence, loud noises of all kinds, especially a woman's scream, and I confess at this point to taking leave of my senses. Once, when I was seven, a neighbor child burst with a horrid bang a balloon just inches from my face. My mother had to forcibly restrain me from pummeling the little baggage, and that insensitive parent even had the temerity to apologize to the brat's mother for *my* behavior.

I struck her again. I must have hit her several times although I do not remember the exact number—my only thought was to still her shrieking horrible voice. I realized after a time that she was quiet and ceased striking her. She looked much less churlish in repose, even somewhat soft and feminine, and this aroused me as it would any man. As she was asleep and couldn't possibly be harmed by my action, I decided to take my pleasure of her. Just as I finished, she had the bad grace to awaken and jumped up, shoving me aside with such violence that my shirt became torn, whereupon she began screeching out the insults and threats I have heretofore mentioned.

This, literally, was the end of my part in the affair. I turned my back on the whore, and she tore off down the river path. A few steps away, while still within earshot I heard her bellow again—oh, nauseous sound! —and I turned just in time to see her clumsy foot trip over a vine and pitch her forward against a large boulder lying partway in the shallows of the river. Her head struck first, sounding much as an egg does when you hurl it at someone's door, as we used to do on Halloween as children. She fell heavily into the water and sank until all that was visible was the blue of her buttocks and a trail of bubbles and froth from her submerged head.

Could I have saved her you ask? Yes, I suppose I could have. There would have been time enough had I been so inclined. It took her body at least ten minutes or so before it worked its way into the heavier current and drifted away. But, pray tell, why should I have? All she had done for me was to plunk her uninvited slut's body down in my space, violate my peace and tranquility, deride and insult me, and then screech like a banshee. For that I am obliged to save her worthless carcass? I rather think not. I didn't push her; she fell of her own accord, or at the least, of her own oafish carelessness, and it was no business of mine that I could see.

I did what any honest man would do; I went about the business I had come there to do. I resumed fishing, although it was useless. As much as I tried to recapture my equanimity and serenity, the cow had thoroughly sabotaged any semblance of restfulness. My day of leisure was destroyed, and I ended up trudging home disconsolately, my entire outing in ruins. You would think that sufficient punishment for my small part in the mishap, but such is not the way of life. Man is like unto the God he has created in his own image; he demands not an eye for an eye, but ten-fold for one. So I sit here, bound for glory as the song is sung and have for companionship, you, my future listener, and this half-eaten, greasy, cheeseburger.

A thought just crossed my mind. Listening to my tale you might assume me bitter, angry. You are mistaken. I am by nature a humble, unassuming man, content to live in a house by the side of the road like Thoreau and let the rest of the world pass by on their frenetic way. I have been caught up in something that is not my doing. I struggle not to be bitter, but you might allow me some leeway in that, considering. All in all, the whole misadventure bores me to distraction. I am not afraid to pass on to the next stage in life nor do I especially or eagerly await it. What can I do about it? Nothing. Exactly nothing whatsoever. Therefore, the intelligent act is to merely wait out the allotted time and then any and all questions will be answered, I presume. (I am speaking of death, if you have not yet comprehended that.) Personally, I believe I will simply cease to exist, or at least my consciousness will, and my physical form will merely change as the lump of coal becomes ashes when burned or a diamond when pressured, even as it was once a tyrannosaurus, but I still cannot deny a slight doubt as to the veracity of that presumption. After all, I really don't know, nor does anyone else so far as I can determine. Look at it this way: forty-four years ago I emerged from a womb into an existence I knew nothing about, and it proved tolerable. I'm sure the next stage will prove much the same. I only hope that no infernal rocking chairs exist in the realm I am to enter nor anyone to hold you prisoner in one.

I am to die at dawn. It will be the last frame of the only film I have a reliable memory of appearing in, the one we agree to term the earthly one. Whether a new one will begin for me upon the termination of the old is a matter that has been debated forever, if we are to believe that pack of formal lies known as recorded history.

Should I choose the firing squad, there will be a dozen or so soldiers in a plumbed line who will follow a series of commands from their superior who will stand slightly to the side and issue orders he is perhaps even now rehearsing before a mirror, trying out different voices to get the most authoritative one.

Then, they will fire their rifles. What is interesting is that not all of the rifles will be loaded with live rounds. One will contain a blank cartridge, filled only with powder, no lethal missile. This is so no one (of the soldiers) will know whose bullet it was that murdered the condemned. This is to salve their consciences, only I have a feeling that most of the participants care not a whit if theirs was the deadly round, and another part of that suspicion is that they will secretly take credit for my death in their own minds. Perhaps there will be arguments over warm beer later. "Yes," one will start, "it was my bullet did him in. I can tell the difference between a live round and a dummy. A live round kicks more . . . and boy, did mine kick! Yes, I am the one who slew him. There is no doubt." This may lead to a fight, as another will chime in. "Yes, I felt the same thing—I know what you're talking about, but your aim is notoriously lousy. You are such a conceit to imagine yours was the bullet. I am the best shot here, and I aimed for the throat, and that is where he was struck the most. That was the wound that killed him. I saw where your bullet struck. Did you see that chip fly off the wall to his left and slightly above his head? There was a large puff of powder and pebbles. That was your bullet, my friend. That is where your bullets always land Monday mornings out on the firing range. Ask the sergeant. High and to the left. Am I right?" This would be addressed to the rest of the assemblage, and the battle would be pitched. It would be interesting to discover who came up with this concept of a blank cartridge. I would think a religious man, a priest. That is the kind of thing they study for, the kinds of moral conundrums they delight in providing.

Or, I may choose the gallows and throw them all into a tizzy. Some will be disappointed and some will feel grateful.

Six-thirty-two is my appointed time to die. That is the time the weather bureau has decreed to be official sunrise, regardless of God, and the great political entity of this state soberly relies on the weather bureau's proclamation as the officious time in which to satisfy Section 911, Sub-Para 11 of the State Penal Code. That's the section dealing with the execution of convicted and justly-sentenced capital-crimes felons.

I die at dawn.

A voice speaks, knocks me out of my reverie.

"Truman."

The turnkey stands before my cell.

"Less than twelve hours, Truman." He smiles not. He is of a mind that he is a serious man and doesn't seem to take pleasure in these announcements, but has an obeisant need to please me for some reason, and he has decided that to tell me how much time I have left is news I am eager for. I am not. Indeed, I care not a whit one way or the other.

I scarcely know him, even though he has been a part of my present situation, i.e., Death Row, for some months now; I am a natural reticent and he seems much the same. At least till this day our conversations for the large part have been sundry and sere. His tone, when announcing the hours I have left, is that of the Queen Mother's emissary announcing an impending presentation to the court with Her Highness on some momentous and grand occasion, most certainly one of a serious mien. I idly wonder if my Maker and the Queen of England and all such in that capacity compare notes on how to receive recalcitrants and if there is a school of such for their turnkeys and heralds or if they learn on the job through a kind of osmosis.

He is gone now, padding away on mushy brown brogans on the wet, cold stones outside my cell.

Earlier, he brought my last meal. They make such a big to-do about that. Three were in attendance: besides my turnkey, two other guards, neither of whom I'd seen before. Sort of the gastronomical committee, I suppose. It was probably a form of titillation for them. Each had a suggestion: two for steak and one for pheasant under glass, which exhibited, in my humble opinion, a lack of imagination and/or intelligence; therefore, to be perverse, I submitted my order for a cheeseburger, French fries and a strawberry shake. Perversity wasn't the sole reason for my selection; that was what I was actually hungry for.

It sits here now, half-eaten. For some reason I have little appetite. I will never admit it to my jailers, but I had a craving for the pheasant after just one nibble of the cheeseburger. It was chilled when I received it, and they had forgotten extra ketchup that I had expressly ordered for the fries. I like to smother them—my secret vice—and looking at them in their cold, naked little bodies angered me although I hid my feelings, and even though they offered to fetch me ketchup from the prison dining room, I had already surrendered my appetite and told them not to bother, not without, I am ashamed to confess, a hint of peevishness in my refusal. I am allowed. It is my last day on earth.

The thing that stands out in my mind about this place is the dampness. Even on the hottest of days, there is a clamminess that persists and soaks into one's bones.

And the noise. It is never quiet, even at four in the

morning. This is a very old prison, much unlike what I understand to be the layout of the modern ones. The Death Row here is not housed in a separate building, nor even in an isolated wing; no, it is simply the top tier of four tiers in this cellblock, which is given the dreary and unimaginative name of "J" Block. A bureaucratic name. No one seems to know what the J stands for, if anything. Below me are the normal inhabitants of any prison. Murderers, thieves, forgers, drug dealers, rapists, a child-molester or two—the usual citizens of this society. Even a cattle rustler I've been told. Never does the mantle of silence descend upon this cellblock. At night, there are screams here and there: men bellowing, I assume from the tone of their yelps, in the throes of passion, while the objects of their affection scream in shrill voices, often for their mothers. At midnight, a train passes by outside and blows its whistle, and the din increases for a period.

Men sobbing. An irritating noise from women, but a patently pathetic sound from men.

Most of the men here loathe the sound of that whistle it would seem, from the curses and cries that emanate from the tiers below. As for myself, I barely notice it, other than the elevated noise level it elicits always wakes me, and that is bothersome. Annoying.

There are three of us on Death Row. The fewest of any place in the country. That is because this state doesn't warehouse condemned men like most others—they do what the court orders and kills us. Me, I prefer this policy. It is straightforward and honest.

I'm in the middle cell. There is an empty cell on either side of mine and then there is my neighbor.

Even though they bring us our meals, we are treated much the same as the other inmates. The only utensil we are allowed is a large, metal soupspoon. They are afraid to let us have a knife or a fork for obvious reasons. We carry the spoon in our back pockets everywhere we go. From time to time, there's a shakedown and they inspect the spoon to make sure we haven't filed the handle down on the concrete floor to sharpen it into a weapon.

They needn't worry about that with me. I'm a peaceful man and have no desire to harm anyone. Except, perhaps, that odious turnkey! (That was a joke, you understand.)

We aren't allowed any detergent to wash our spoon with and can only rinse it in the small sink in our cell.

We eat beans for every meal, including breakfast. You have to bite down carefully and slowly on each spoonful. The warden has an allowance for our food and if he can save money from his allotted budget, he is allowed to keep the savings for himself. Beans are the cheapest foodstuff he can purchase, so it's included on the menu for every repast.

The reason you have to bite down carefully is that the merchants sell the beans to him in one-hundred-pound burlap bags. They're sold by the weight. Therefore, they always include a shovelful of gravel in each bag. They cheat the warden and the warden cheats us. That's where it ends, as there isn't anyone below us that we can cheat. The buck stops here, so to speak.

The inmate cooks don't bother to sort out the gravel. They're criminals, not master chefs, and therefore possess no pride in their craft.

On my first day in here, I bit down on a rock and cracked a molar in half. I haven't been to see the dentist about it as I'd already heard the tales about the medical care in here. They're either Third World refugees with questionable degrees from Caribbean schools, or they've got drug or alcohol habits. The state doesn't pay them much, so most supplement their incomes by selling the drugs in their possession to inmates. The Novocain the dentist uses is an anesthetic in name only. It's mostly distilled water from what I've been told, and I consider the information reliable.

I've grown accustomed to the throbbing and rarely even notice it by now. Even if the dentist here were a Park Avenue professional performing some kind of charity act by administering to convicts once a week and had the finest of drugs, I wouldn't have him look at it or fix it. What for? I'm going to die anon. How possibly would it profit me if I were to die without a toothache? I don't think I'll be fearful when my time comes, but if for some reason I am, the ache in my jaw will take my mind off of my impending fate a bit, perhaps. Or not. We shall see.

We who are on Death Row are afforded somewhat larger cells than those in the general population. There are no windows in the backs of our cells, and there are solid walls separating us on each side from our neighbors. I look across to the far wall at a barred window that overlooks the yard in the center of the prison, but I can't see anything but the sky as we are too high and the windows are above me. If I stand at the cell door, I can see part of the walkway directly in front of my cell and perhaps a foot or two to each side. I see the railing on the walk, but we are too high to see the ground floor where the cellblock guard sits at his desk from our cells. I can hear the guards when they walk by. Their shoes have a heavy sound, very distinct. When other inmates pass by, theirs is a decidedly softer sound. The shoes the state issues us have more of a crepe sole, not exactly like a tennis shoe, but softer than the leather of the guards' footwear, which is more of a boot. Except for that turnkey. His step sounds more like ours.

Ours squeak when they are wet.

The turnkey also has a maddening habit of clacking his master key on all the cell bars as he passes. Other inmates sometimes scream at him to stop his infernal clatter, but he either ignores them or perhaps has simply zoned them out of his consciousness.

I will tell you a story that illustrates how I feel about leaving this life. I had an acquaintance my own age who passed on last year, his ticket out being cancer of some obscure part of the body. He had lived a fast-paced life, moving here, then there, working at first at this profession, then that, cohabiting with this person, then that one, sleeping very little so that he could cram "experiences" into his day. In short, he led a very active life. When I visited him, he cried and blubbered and said he couldn't bear to die yet; there was so much he had left to do and not enough time to do it in—he felt he'd scarcely been alive five minutes. I pondered this when I left his bedside. I was the same age, had done not one one-hundredth of the things he had, but yet I felt as if I had lived forever and could die at any time with a full and rich life behind me. Isn't that sad, that he had done so much in the way of amusements and adventures while I had scarcely any, but my life was stuffed and complete and his but a flash of light, a minor super-nova, that had sped by in a blink? Quality, not quantity, has been the cornerstone of my life and if I were to feel pity, which I assure you I do not, it would be for my acquaintance, not for myself.

You think me cold for not mourning the man? Let me tell you about cold. I smoke unfiltered Camel cigarettes. Many times, I have had total strangers approach me and say, "Say there, you shouldn't smoke those. They will kill you straightaway." Or some other such blather. Were they warm, caring human beings concerned with my health and welfare? To be sure, on the surface it appears so, especially to one unsophisticated in the ways of mankind, but no, not a bit. We were unknown to each other, and even if we had been acquainted and they, in fact, detested me, they would have uttered the same mawkish sentiments. What they were really saying was, "Look, I feel I am superior to you because I don't have that filthy habit, and I want you to be aware that I am not only better than you but infinitely more intelligent. You can die tomorrow for all I really care. Just recognize how vastly superior I am." They make this big show to others to demonstrate their love for humanity, when all they truly feel is contempt for what they perceive to be a weakness they aren't afflicted with. Do you really feel they are caring folk? Of course you do, for you say the same things yourself. Do you see how silly your definition of "caring" is now? Well, of course you don't. You cannot see past the words to the motive.

I, on the other hand, would never presume to offer unsolicited advice to another. They have their business and their life, and I have no business mucking about in it. Why set myself up as some sort of a know-it-all who presumes to know what's best for others? And yet people do just that, always and always, and consider themselves to be caring, compassionate folk, when the truth is I am a thousand times more the humanitarian. I do not stoop to meddle in other's lives. I deliver them the respect I wish afforded me. Can you tell me of another more honest than I? I think not. Make your own conclusions of this.

Here comes that damnable turnkey again. I wonder what precious pearls of wisdom or scintillating tidbits of conversation he has to offer this time. *What's that? Ten hours to go. Why thank you my good man. Am I to understand you will be by here each and every hour on the stroke to give me this priceless information? You will? That makes me so happy that I cannot express with my poor vocabulary the ecstasy that knowledge brings. And you, too, sir. You have a nice day also!*

Damnable cur! In the whole of my life I have not once wished for one single, lonely thing, except for this: I wish I were to be executed in an electric chair instead of by firing squad and that my dear friend, the turnkey, would keep me company at that time by sitting in my lap.

And I lied. I am surprised that I said that to you. About never once wishing for something. At one time in my life I did yearn for something. Some well-meaning but misdirected acquaintance (actually, it was my barrister—I wonder what his ulterior motive was?) convinced me, against my better judgment, that I would be well served by taking a holiday. It is the only one I have ever permitted myself or suffered through, and looking back I should have followed my own instincts and remained home. I must confess that in perusing the brochures and listening to them extol the virtues of the Bahama Islands, I experienced a tiny surge of pleasant anticipation, but stupidly I forgot that I was ensconced at the time comfortably in my sitting room and not actually feeling the scorching sun in the photographs. I became convinced that this excursion would be the happiest event of my life, and, yes, I did earnestly and avidly ache for the day to arrive when I could depart on my adventure.

My sabbatical was to take the space of an entire month. It was dreadful. I endured but one week before I returned. It was then I underwent the excruciating and unfamiliar sense of desiring something so badly I could, to use a vulgar and common expression, "almost taste it." And what was the object of this desperate longing? Simply, just one small hour in one of our fall downpours. I lusted after it, the feel of a day like that. You know the kind: the wind is brisk, coppery, the wet chill gnawing pleasantly at your joints, everything is black and gray and your bones are raw and bloodless. That is a feeling! That is weather that is honest! That is weather that excites! The sun in the islands is boring, insipid, the sun of women. The same, day after day after interminable day. I went mad. When home I arrived, after a swirl of airplanes and taxicabs, of panic urgency in the hands of tortoise-like public conveniences, I knelt down on trembling knee and kissed the damp, dear sod. Emotions new to my body swept through me as I tarried there, blessing the icy mist that whipped the sleeves of my outer coat and sent my teeth clacking in a happy chatter. My nose ran and the tears froze upon my cheeks as I knelt there, long, delicious minutes, savoring the splendid rain, and never—never, I repeat—have I felt more alive and well with the world.

So you see, I lied. I *have* wished for something before, but it was a lie of omission and that only because I had forgotten it.

My trial. An absolute mockery. A sham. I am sorry not to use more colorful adjectives, but these two words describe what transpired better than two thousand others might.

I acted as my own attorney. I entered the affair knowing the outcome already, understanding society as I do, and what need was there to waste perfectly good money on someone who could only prolong the inevitable and bore me to tears by making me recite again and again the events of the day to be examined? No need at all. I must admit with some pride that although I had never before been inside a courtroom previous to that day, I quitted myself handsomely.

My presentation of the facts was crisp and concise, not to mention unbiased and exact, my vocabulary exquisite and my delivery oratorical: at moments it soared to poetical heights. As proof, I offer an overheard exchange, whispered from some unknown spectator to another, in hushed, reverent tones, a complicated comparison of my stentorian ejaculations to that of the renowned Mr. Clarence Darrow, and, while I held admirable control of my emotions throughout the trial, I flushed with pride at this bit of accidental praise.

The prosecutor was a stunted scrap of a man, creeping and evil, blacksuited like a shiny beetle, and bent upon improving his political career at my expense. No matter that; it is the way of the world. He won the case, as any simpleton would have, but in the doing was exposed as a shallow, posturing simp, contrasted as he was forced to be against my own brilliance in oratory. I am positive my eloquence was not expected; a glimpse of his jaw dropping in awe at my erudition when first I began to speak brought a smile to my lips. My emotions were akin to the person the mugger holds a shining knife to the throat of who refuses to turn over his money as a point of honor. Even as dozens of people swirl about the sidewalks around the mugger and his victim, many of them excited at the possible bloodletting, so did my fellow villagers seated in the courtroom view me. I was just such a victim, in that courtroom, the base villagers surrounding me, my death assured but my spirit undaunted and soaring against those puny nobodies. Death—what is death? I asked the prosecutor, straight out. Is this what you see to threaten me with, scare me? Boo! I exclaimed to those in attendance. Use that word to frighten your children, such as I will fling it back in your faces, for death holds no alarm nor value for me, no more than it does for any brave resister. I take life as it comes, never stepping aside for such as these, no matter the consequence to my safety, and we live as we shall someday die, eyes open and head erect, and do what you will, it matters not. You have your knife at my throat and I laugh at you. It is you that are afraid, not I; even though you manage to murder me you will still be afraid of me the day after I am lowered into the ground. You will dream of me when you are alone in your beds at night and wake in cold drops of sweat, your heart palpitating and your eyes large and round and luminous in the sterile beam of the moon. This and other such remarks I made to the prosecutor and the room at large, and there was silence for a long moment after I spoke.

It was foregone that he should win a conviction, so the victory was no victory, save for a straw-snatcher such as he. A hollow win, on points, after being on the ropes for the entire bout. Our match was over fair before it had begun.

Every sentence he uttered was a lie of one sort or the other; as for me, I remained on the side of truth no matter the cost or pain.

Yes, I hit her.

Yes, I fucked her.

Don't say that word again, said the judge.

I will use any word I choose, said I. It's a fine, Anglo-Saxon word that means exactly what it sounds like, unlike the prissy French and Latin you employ in this room that deflect from the truth at angles and never hit it straight on. I went on, ignoring his stunned face with its lack of intelligence anywhere in his features.

Yes, she enticed me.

Yes, I saw her fuck three others willingly.

Yes, she was a harlot.

Yes, she slipped and fell, striking her head.

Yes, she drowned.

Yes, I could have saved her.

No, I didn't try to save her.

And like that, ad infintum.

On and on it went, interminably. The trial wasted three days; by eleven o'clock of the first day, I was done with it. The facts had been presented; they could have stopped the farce at this junction, passed sentence and been done with it. But no, the *law* must be satisfied, and they must go over the same dreary, mind-numbing details until you want to scream or gag or beat your chest, anything to relieve the tedium this great principality requires to consider a circus a trial.

It became so excruciatingly dull that I resorted to picking my nose and eating the snot, with exaggerated gestures, in full view of all, and farting loudly whenever the opportunity arose. Give the peasants a howl, you know. When the judge reprimanded me, face red as a Bahamian sun and eyebrows a'bristle as he stammered out his admonishment, I sneered and pointed out that not only was my behavior assuredly not uncivilized—the old Celtic kings behaved in like manner when exhibiting their disdain for the lower creatures surrounding them—it was my right, if not duty, as a gentleman to comport myself in this manner, considering the company I found myself amid, moral precedent having been well-established.

That unnerved him absolutely. He fixed me with a weak, nelly stare, but it was clear to all present that I was his better and had triumphed.

When finally it came time to pass sentence, I stood proudly at the docket, posture erect, suit cleaned and pressed to a military crease, and stared the judge royally in the eye. It was *his* hand that trembled, *his* gaze that wavered as he spoke the words, "...have been found guilty and are hereby sentenced to death by firing squad or the gallows upon your election," on such and such a day and at such and such a time at such and such a place, blah, blah, blah. You recognize the form.

What? I cannot hear you turnkey. You have to speak louder, from the diaphragm. Oh yes, ten hours is it? Well, thank you, I am sure. What? Again, you speak too lowly. No. No, thank you. I want to look at them and marvel at what civilization has risen to. You have a nice day too, sir.

Wait a minute. Hold on there. Come here, sir. I'll tell you what. Take the fries and leave the cheeseburger. I am afraid gazing upon too many of these culinary achievements will frazzle my brain, and I shall grow dizzy with wonder. And you might fetch me a cup of that syrup you call coffee. I wonder what the Colombians might think of your handiwork with the fruits of their labor. Black, please... like my soul. Ha-ha.

There. You see? I shall be filled with joy when ten hours has elapsed. There is a man, two cells from mine on the left, whose date is in three months. Can you imagine? The man on my right, also two cells away, has six months remaining. Three... *six* more months of staring at and listening to the turnkey? I think of him (the turnkey) as Mr. Timex. He's cheap and no matter what, he keeps on a'tickin'.

Do you know why they keep an empty cell between each of we condemned men and me? It is so we cannot conspire to do each other in. That would be breaking the law and a poor example for other felons, not to mention ordinary citizens. A very serious crime indeed! It is considered a vile thing to try and cheat the firing squad in this principality. I am not sure what the penalty is, if it is a stiff fine or something more corporeal, but I am convinced it to be severe, the way in which they speak of it. Always we are told we will "be in serious trouble" were we to attempt suicide, and I dread thinking of the punishment should we succeed!

Just think. If you were the one to assist your fellow doomed prisoner in such an endeavor, they would first punish you by delaying your execution date for at least another six months or so while they try you on the new charge. Imagine! Six additional months of listening to Mr. Timex! If only they would realize that no one in a sane state of mind would risk such a fate!

I dream. I dream, and out of my dream comes a plan of genius. I was once able to fly.

Before you laugh, listen. When I am done, tell me that in all rectitude you have not done the same thing, or, if you be as honest with yourself as you claim to be, tell me that somewhere in your own illusions you do not remember doing as I have done. We shall see, by and by.

When I was a child, we lived for the space of a few months in another house that was situated in a kind of housing project, dozens of ticky-tacky houses, one like the next, in row after row of pastel-colored boxes, each exactly a copy of its neighbor. Some repairs were being done to our own home, I believe, which required we live in this dwelling. Each block of the project was on a hillside; that is, the house at the head of the block was higher than the last house on the opposite end. The front yards slanted evenly throughout, but the back yards, ah, the back yards! Here is where the project architect snuck in some creativity. Each lot had a steep drop to the next, like steps in the Great Pyramid. What of it, you say? Well, it was because of this physical anomaly that I discovered I could aviate. One day, around the age of six, I jumped from my back yard down into that of our neighbor's. Purely by chance, I found myself not falling, as had always been the case before, but rather, I *floated.* Agitated beyond belief at this discovery, I attempted the feat again, this time with negative results. Rather than pass it off as a once-in-a-lifetime miracle, I strained again and again to reconstruct the elements of the event, failing miserably in my goal each time. All I succeeded in accomplishing was to become exhausted and discouraged. The many attempts had numbed me, both physically and emotionally, by the time I made my final attempt, and it was on this final leap that I again experienced the elation I had on the first chance victory over gravity. I floated! I was euphoric, elated, beside myself! The secret, I discovered at that precise moment, was not in any particular body position, wind currents, or air temperatures, but came strictly from a mindset. It was a combination of the way I arranged my thoughts and a form of breath control that enabled me to ignore the physical law of gravity, allowing me to float above the ground for so long as I desired. I simply used my will to make my body a collection of cells lighter than air and held my breath, or nearly so; I could allow tiny amounts of oxygen to pass back and forth, enough to sustain life.

That was but part of the trick. It is complicated, but I will try to explain how I did it so that you might understand. To be successful at floating, all superfluous thought had to be expunged from my mind. I could think, but with another part of my brain. In essence, I had to split my brain into two parts. The central part, or part I was used to using, had to be sent into a sort of suspension where no thought, no electrical impulses could occur, and a new part of my brain, which before now I hadn't known existed, came into use, and with this new part I could do anything, think anything, break physical and chemical laws at will. At first, I used it solely to direct my flight, soaring higher and loftier as my confidence in these abilities grew.

Initially, I could only hover for a few seconds at best, but as I learned to harness my new power, the length of my flights increased as did the distances I was able to rise to. I began jumping off higher and higher hills and then one day found I was able to rise into the air while standing on level ground.

This continued until the age of eleven when I suddenly lost the power. I forget the occasion, it obviously has been suppressed by my subconscious, but I do know the reason I could no longer fly. When I placed myself into this state, a kind of self-hypnosis I imagine, I also put myself at risk with my environment, the chief enemy becoming other human beings. To wit: I began to realize that if my concentration were broken while aloft, I would plummet to the ground. From the first, that fear was present in the back of my thoughts, and as I became more and more adept and skilled at wingless flight and therefore more able to open my mind up to more and diverse mental activity, the realization of my danger became more and more apparent. This would prove to be the death-knell of my new ability. In short, I learned to fear. And wingless flight by a human is completely dependent upon the total absence of fear. Once that element is introduced into the mind, then further flight is impossible.

As I say, I don't recall the exact instance that ended my floating adventures. It may have been that someone saw me while being borne aloft and frightened me by shouting, or it may have been something else, such as the discovery of a new interest that captured my interest and imagination, such as one in the opposite sex, but whatever the cause, I lost the power. And the longer I went before attempting to exercise it, the more the power atrophied. First, I lost the ability to take off from a flat spot, and then I could no longer remain airborne when leaping from a hill, and I became as stuck to the planet as everyone else.

Oh, I knew there was a way back, rather, I vaguely realized what it would take to regain my magic, but I also knew I was no longer capable of doing what was required. For the power insists on suspension of all fears and laying yourself open to the actions of others. Pure trust and utter guilelessness must be achieved, and I felt that to be impossible any longer, for I had passed into a terrible state wherein that was no longer feasible. I had become an adult.

I suspect that is what Christ is mystically saying when he tells the Pharisee he must become as a "little child" again.

There was another power I possessed as a child, recently recalled as well, and that was the ability to leave my body and hover above it. I only did this at night, when everyone was asleep and not likely to walk in and disturb me whilst unconnected to my body. I knew from the beginning that such an interruption would prove fatal and that I would either perish outright or forever be estranged from my flesh, a prospect that terrified me. I believe I ceased leaving my body at about the same time I ceased flying and for exactly the same reasons. I am sure I was eleven years old at this time. About to turn twelve. Unlike Christ at the same age, I felt no call to proselytize, my main activity at this period becoming an intense desire to satisfy my carnal nature. I self-abused my flesh, incessantly.

I grow skittish. Do you know the sensation? It is the feeling you get when you imbibe caffeine to excess or stay up studying for final exams and consume handfuls of NoDoze or other stimulants, or perhaps *you* feel skittish at moments of crisis. Could that be the culprit in this case? Now, I mean, for me, in this situation? Just because I sit here calmly and think that things are the same as always, does part of my brain see my impending execution as a kind of predicament and therefore produce excess adrenaline?

Here is what I have thought in the last moment. Note this, for I feel it important: the difference between Europeans and Americans is that Americans think in terms of dialogue; Europeans, especially the Gauls, are the only ones capable of linear thought (Germans don't count—they think in terms of machines, in terms of monologue). Do you see? That thought is totally unrelated to what we have been talking about. It's like when the husband rushes to the hospital to see his wife whom he's just learned has been struck by an automobile; he dashes to her bedside and stands there, coat still on, face red from exertion and emotion, lungs heaving, and perspiration drying on his reddened forehead as he gazes at her still, unconscious form, bandages covering everything but one dark aperture where her left eye should be, and his mind can only come up with one image. All he can think of is the advertisement he saw in passing in yesterday's newspaper, offering green peas for only thirty-nine cents per can. He cannot rid his mind of that tableau, which is doubly preposterous since he detests peas and never eats them. He feels as though he should rush out and buy a can of those peas quickly, or something dire will transpire. And then new moisture forms on his brow, and it is not the honest sweat of running to catch a broken wife, but the salty liquid of a guilty man's skin when he thinks God is snooping into his thoughts and will sentence him to Hell for not thinking of his wife at this crisis, instead daydreaming of a fatuous tin of vegetables. It is as though a choice must be made, right now, and he is being pulled against his will to make the wrong one. He is beside himself with worry now and cannot erase the image of the peas. It grows stronger the more he tries to shake it; now he can even smell them and more; he can taste their odious flavor, and God's heavy breath is hot on his neck, and he looks at his wife, eyes unblinking in a panic because suddenly he cannot now remember her first name.

Where were we? Oh yes, the details of my crime…

I was brought to this prison straightway. The authorities said they feared for my life. A lynching by my fellow townspeople was mentioned. There was some big talk in the village square and at Joe's Tavern that hanging was too good for me. Several favored castration. I suppose so that I couldn't rape anyone in the next life if I went into it with this equipment. They aren't very intelligent, my neighbors, and if the authorities had only consulted with me they would have learned that put together there isn't half a man with the nerve to do what they proposed while alcohol moved their tongues. They are all gas and wind and of no substance whatsoever. A brisk wind would have knocked down all their sails. One stout policeman would have dispersed them like minnows before a bloodthirsty pickerel.

It mattered very little to me. In truth, I preferred it here to that tiny lean-to they choose to call a jail in New Haven. Here, at the prison, I have room to stretch my limbs and a library (scantily stocked, but still with a book or two) to browse about in; I have a turnkey who tells me the time and fetches me coffee-swill when I order it; in truth, my existence is that of a royal prince compared to what I received at the jail in New Haven.

I had been here one day short of a week when the chief warder had me brought to his office. It was a room like him. They say that dogs and their masters begin to resemble each other after a time; this man and his room had come to the same situation. It was a musty green, olive in tone, with dusty books lying about in a haphazard fashion. After I got to know Lars (the warden), I learned that his mind was equally disorderly. He had some semblance of intelligence, and he had read a book or two, though virtually none I would consider worthy of more than a flip through. Except one or two authors. Who? Well, you know that he is my jailer—that should be clue enough to tell you what Russian he was enamored of and what French novelist whose name begins with a G he also invested his leisure time in.

Physically, he was fuzzy, his voice thick and slurred, and furry, like a 78 record played at 33 1/3 speed, and his face was indistinct, out-of-focus. He reminded me of the cinema star, Brian Keith. He put me on edge with his manner of speaking, slowly and deliberately, as if each word that passed his lips was an aircraft carrier he was launching. I wanted to finish his sentences for him, and I had the uneasy feeling that time was speeding by and we were falling into another dimension. He created the sensation Dorothy must have felt at the beginning of the

Wizard of Oz when she begins her journey.

"Truman Pinter," he started, when I had seated myself. I observed the chair I was sitting in to be the same color as my mother's rocking chair; his also, a detail that set my stomach aboil.

"I see by your file that you were educated at Princeton." What this had to do with my incarceration and sentence escaped me. Did he suppose I was the first graduate from that distinguished center of study to run afoul of the law? I remained silent, waiting for something meaty to respond to. Idle conversation is not my suit. I saw no advantage nor good use of my time in parroting confirmation of a fact he had in indisputable black and white before him.

"I, too, graduated from that university."

I was supposed to be impressed? Many thousands have graduated from Princeton, although I suspect not many of them have become prison wardens. I wondered what those who care about such things thought about his choice of careers.

"Some of my officers think that's humorous."

"Do you think that as well?" I asked. I couldn't stop the smile that came to my lips.

"I think..." He half-rose, his voice a storm erupting. "I think...you're an animal, but more than an animal. You're the worst kind of animal. A highly educated man who has no morals. You know, we have all kinds of criminals in here, but what almost all of them have in common is a deprived background of one form or another. When I see someone like yourself, who has had the best of everything, I find I have very little regard for that person. While nothing can forgive criminality, at least these other men have something of an excuse. What I think is that the time can't pass quickly enough before the world is rid of your kind."

He settled back down into his chair and seemed to gain some sort of control over himself. It was obvious it took some effort. He spoke again after a moment or two, which time he spent picking up various papers from the piles on his desk and rearranging them into other piles.

"I am, however, fascinated by several parts of your crime, although my instincts are to avoid your loathsome presence. I find I have another motive in doing so in that I feel death to be too little a punishment for what you have done and for the sort of monster you are. Considering your advantages."

He paused again, clasped his hands together on the desk and smiled at me.

"So what I've decided to do, since you don't seem to be affected by the threat of death, is do what little I can to make your remaining days . . . shall we say, less comfortable?" His smile turned into an outright grin.

"For starters, I have reason to believe you're suicidal. I'm putting your guards on a suicide watch."

I knew what that meant. Every hour, twenty-four hours a day, a guard would come by and check on me. At night, he'd shine a bright flashlight over my face. It meant the end of what little privacy I still possessed. Worse, it meant it would be difficult to continue my practice sessions. Practice for my escape.

"I'm not the least suicidal," I said. "And you know it."

"That's not what it says here," he said, that silly grin still on his face. He picked up one of the papers he had been moving from pile to pile and held it up. "This is a report from one of the guards on the Row. He says he's observed you staring at your razor for long moments while you shave. If that isn't direct evidence of a suicide wish, I don't know what is."

So that was the way it was going to be, I thought. Very well then, I decided. I wouldn't give him the satisfaction of knowing this turn of events bothered me in the remotest. I'd still be able to practice, albeit it was going to be more difficult. Still, I could manage. I smiled back at him, a benign, passive smile.

"It will be good to have the company," I said. "Many times at night I get to feeling somewhat lonely. You have done me a favor, and I appreciate it. It will be lovely to have someone to share a smoke with and some conversation during the night."

His reaction was what I should have expected. He added another punishment.

"I don't think so," he said, losing his toothy smile for just an instant. It crept back slowly as he seemed to have an inspiration. "Your smoking privileges are canceled. I'm afraid you may injure yourself from the match flame or the cigarette itself. This is all for your own good, you know," he added, standing up to indicate the interview was over.

"There are so many things I have to thank you for," I said, maintaining my own smile. "I've wanted to quit the filthy habit for a very long time and now you've given me the opportunity to do so. I have heard some of the inmates and even some of the guards say that you were an inhumane man, even going so far as to call you vile names. Now I know they are wrong. You are the most humane of men. I only wish I had made your acquaintance many years ago. You might have been able to 'save me from myself', as they say. I appreciate these little efforts you're making on my behalf, and, believe me, they won't go unrewarded in the afterlife. Not if there is a true God!" I rose myself and offered him my hand.

"Out!" he said, his voice raised and angry. "Get the hell out of my office. Guard!" The guard responded immediately from his post just outside the door. "Take this man back to his cell and confiscate his cigarettes."

As we were leaving, he said to my back, more softly this time but with a detectable note of glee, "Oh, Pinter, I'm very sorry, but I believe we went over on our appointment, and the men have already been served supper. I apologize for being responsible for your missing your meal."

I turned, just as we reached the door. "Again, Warden, I am in your debt. How did you know I have been thinking about my weight? Just this morning I had vowed to eliminate one meal a day. I just didn't know which one

I wanted to eliminate. Now, you've made that decision for me. Thank you again." And I turned and walked out ahead of the guard, my demeanor calm on the outside but seething inside.

The guard that escorted me back to the Row came back shortly after he had locked me down and handed me two stale dinner rolls through the bars.

"Here," he said in a gruff tone, not meeting my eyes. "A man shouldn't starve just because somebody's an asshole."

"I don't want it," I said, placing the offering on the floor outside my cell. "I'm trying to lose a few pounds and the warden was nice enough to assist me in my goal." There was just the chance the warden had put the guard up to this, to see if he had actually gotten to me. If I accepted the gift, he'd know he had me. The guard shrugged his shoulders and picked up the rolls. "Suit yourself, buddy," he said, walking away. "One asshole deserves another, I guess."

The very next day, I was summoned to the green room once again. This time, I identified something in his appearance that had bothered me the previous visit but which had eluded me when I tried to identify the source of vexation. It was his eyebrows. Eyebrows have always been a feature of interest to me. If the eyes are the windows of the soul, the eyebrows are the weathervanes. And, Lars' eyebrows were that, weathervanes. They were the sort that predicted the hurricane or the calm. If they were lying down, it was safe to go sailing.

If they were bristly and quivering, it was best to head to port. Right now, they were shooting out at every angle, like a porcupine's quills when he faces a maddened bear. If I read them correctly, a dark, ugly storm was brewing. I was right. The storm broke before I had time to sit.

"I don't understand you!" he thundered, the blood in his temples threatening to burst from their pipelines. The guard who had escorted me to his office backed up and exited with white, tight lips, as if it had been he whom his superior was shouting at. The door closed quickly behind him with nothing but a careful click. The outburst had startled me, but my face feigned indifference. I seated myself and crossed my legs. I flicked a nonexistent speck of lint from my prison denims.

"What don't you understand?"

He sat down in his own chair, throwing his body into it like a sack of potatoes purchased at too dear a price, his desk between us like a moat. A jumble of books cut off half his upper body from my view. A volume of Jung caught my eye. Was that for show, I wondered, or had he crept into those pages? The brief flicker of respect was doused when I spied a Cliff's Notes on the same book beneath it.

"I'm a graduate of Princeton myself. You know, I'm not naive enough to suppose all my fellow alumni to be of noble character, but I have never been able to understand sodomy or bestiality, among the usual sort of men we get in here, and I absolutely cannot understand it in one such as you! And if I were to understand those acts, there exists no provision for understanding a man who would force a large stick into someone and break it off inside."

There it was. He was a Freudian and in the worst sense. Probably didn't even realize it. The orifice chosen in my crime was all-important to him, in his scheme of life. And my choice reflected on his alma mater in some convoluted manner. He had arranged his universe into a complicated set of totems, and someone had rearranged one of them, and now all his dominoes were in danger of tumbling down. He was a moron. No, worse. He was a Yale grad.

"You could stand me better if I'd chosen the more usual orifice?" I offered, feeling pity for him and holding out to him the opportunity to realize his mistake. "Or, if I had attended another school, preferably a state university somewhere in the Midwest?"

Sparks flew from his eyebrows. "You're a purely evil person. An abomination." He stood and thrust his finger at me, his gesture like the kiss of Judas upon me. "I've always hated executions we hold. This is one I wouldn't miss, believe me."

I offered no clue to my feelings, giving only a shrug of my shoulders. I was at the whim of whatever caprice his mind invented. I was very much aware that I was the prisoner.

"I'm sorry," he said after a moment, casting down his eyes, a blush tingeing his complexion. He fiddled with some papers on his desk, their rustling the only sound in the room. He acted as if his monomaniac cant had never occurred, or that it had been inconsequential, a small matter, like some mildly cross words to a friend. I could not follow his comings and goings, his mood changes, the extreme emotional poles he swung back and forth between. I pushed my chair an inch or two away from the desk and waited for his next words.

"I see by your record here that you were trained to be a teacher. Of English. Why is it you never taught?"

Who could guess his thought patterns? I gave up trying.

"I liked teaching. I detested children."

I elaborated, as that seemed to be what he wanted. "By the age of five, children labor under the assumption they know everything worth knowing. Who knows? They may have something there. The odd thing is, the ones that feel they know the most end up with one hand on a Standard Oil gasoline pump with their name stitched over their shirt pocket and their other hand scratching their testicles, their evenings employed in watching Wheel of Fortune and wishing Vanna White would drop by their house after the show and sit on their face. If you were to bring up the name Camus in their company, they would assume you were mispronouncing a myopic cartoon character's name, thereby proving your ignorance to them and embellishing their notion that educated persons have no horse sense, the only real intelligence worth having, in their enlightened view. In that tiny piece of their head they cavalierly term their brain, they see the world through the amber shades of a Budweiser. One such person is intolerable; a room filled with thirty-five such aberrations is an invitation to madness. Being another gooey Mr. Chips is not an ambition that ever befell me, thank you."

He looked goggle-eyed, like a bullfrog with a cheek full of flies, one of which doesn't taste quite right.

"You hate everything, don't you?"

I regarded him. Such a little man. In mind, as well as in stature. He sat there, in his olive-green corduroy three-piece suit with the black tie, a small, crumpled lump of flesh. Even from where I sat I could see clumps of hair sticking out of his fleshy ears and his bulbous nose.

"You don't have to answer that," he went on. "I can see by your face I've hit a nerve. And if that weren't enough, I have your record to verify my opinion. There's nothing in there that suggests any trace of a relationship with anyone except possibly your parents, and my guess is that was only out of necessity. I'll bet the only time you've ever had sex was with the girl you find yourself in here for, the one you raped and killed."

"I didn't kill her!" I would give anything to have kept from saying that and with that much vehemence, but it came out before I could think.

"Oh? Is that right? Well, I guess we'd better reconvene the judge and jury then, because they all agreed that you had. It looks like there's been a terrible mistake that's been made, Pinter." He flashed his insufferable grin once more.

"I've already admitted to her rape," I said, getting myself under control. "If you want to call what happened a rape. But I didn't kill her. She killed herself."

"Yeah," he said, sarcasm dripping from his voice and evident in his face, "I've heard your line of reasoning on that before. You really believe that crap, don't you?"

I stood up. "I believe it because it's the truth." I pushed my chair in toward the desk and straightened up, looking him dead in the eye. "If you want to execute me for raping the girl, then go ahead. I don't care. But when you punish me for breaking your law of murder then you are in error. You've changed the meaning of murder, the definition, to suit your purposes. I'll let you kill me, just as you thirst to," I said, my anger barely under control, "but under my terms, not yours. When you finally do bring an end to my existence, the knowledge of my innocence will follow you all the days of your life. As it will my jury and my judge."

"What do you mean, under *your* terms?" He rose and walked over to stand a few inches in front of me. "Are you really planning on suicide?"

I hoped he could see the contempt in my eyes that blazed inside. "No, you idiot. I don't have to commit suicide to beat you. You think that death will defeat me, but death is nothing, only a little space between this world and the next. But *I'll* choose the time of my death in such a way that you'll know dying doesn't concern me in the least, and you'll also know that society has erred in placing this sentence on me. I want to go back to my cell now, if you please."

He walked back to his chair and sat down. "We have a new foreman for your execution, Pinter, a gentleman I'm to meet with tomorrow. Perhaps he will allow me the honor in your case." His eyes gleamed and his eyebrows stood at attention. "And you will go when I dismiss you. Sit down, Pinter. I'm not finished with you just yet."

I did as he said, knowing it was useless to protest, but I took the initiative. I know what he wanted. My soul.

"Do you know, Warden, that this country ranks third in the world in the percentage of its citizens it locks up? Only Russia and South Africa have more of their people under lock and key. Both of their governments have been overthrown. Doesn't that scare you as a member of the ruling apparatus? There's a warning there that I know escapes you, sir. What do you think your fate is to be as a member of the ruling class that chooses repression over reform?"

He had no answer for that. I waited for one, but since none seemed forthcoming, I went on, utilizing the opportunity to set him straight.

"You seek my feelings here, is that correct, Mr. Big-Shot Warden, Mr. Princeton Graduate? You are familiar with the particulars, at least the popular version bandied about by the press and have read the transcript of my trial, so I can only presume your interest lies in my emotions. I am sorry to disappoint. You would want me to feel contrition? Or perhaps dread at the approaching hour? You feel that as the time nears, you will be witness to sweaty palms, labored breathing, a glaze in the eye? Maybe a last-minute blathering to some ghost-god in the sky, begging mercy with foam on my lips?

"I see it in your eyes. You're like a cat observing a mouse. You think the mouse does not know you are there or why you wait, but I have a surprise for you. This mouse is not a mouse, but a lion, and therefore capable of but one emotion: disdain. He cares not for your purpose. He sneers at your purpose. He is as the eagle, watching the watcher, knowing he is in command. The dragonfly watches the mosquito, the fish watches the dragonfly, the osprey watches the fish, and the eagle watches the osprey. Where are you in the chain? I tell you now I am the eagle and there is none higher in the chain. I think it is your hands that shall become wet. We shall see. We'll go on with our game, you and I, since that is what you want, and to be truthful, it amuses me as well.

"I know what it is you truly want..."

Without warning, he raised his arm above his head and smote the table that separated us. The hair in his nostrils flared like a flower opening her petals. "Enough!" he shouted.

My voice was low and confident when I spoke. "You seek understanding. You have a great fear that I am right in the way I view existence, and if that is true then you are a farce and your life with it. A great sweat boils in your brain at the possibility, waiting in dread for a proof that will show you to have been a lie, hoping that my words or actions will trip me up and make me the charlatan, not you. You are doomed to disappointment, and in that lies your hell, and it is that which you fear. You pretend love and compassion for all creatures and claim that is the basis for your interest, knowing in your secret black soul that such feelings are a fabrication of a restless humanity, never attainable simply because there is no such thing. I am Truth, the only truth you have darted to encounter."

And you are looking out of hell, not into it when your eyes lock with mine.

I saw an unholy light flare in his eyes and knew he'd received my thought. A look of pure horror passed over his features, and then he shook his head briefly, violently, as if to shake away what had just passed between us.

He just sat there, a lump in his chair, struck dumb by my eloquence. He wants a game, I thought; I'll give him such a game as he'll wish he'd never entered the fray.

"See? Your upper lip gleams with moisture. Ha-ha! Let us go on. I have cast my plug and you see it. Part of you is in fear and part is mesmerized. I am a different kind of fisherman than you know. You will recognize me at the end, but it will be too late. You are too dense to see it. My bait is out there, swirling against the current; I do not retrieve it. It is not my way. I will allow you to execute me, as I say, but it will be done in such a time as I decree, not you, and that is all I'll say about that. Remember our conversation, sir. One day you will remember this and know."

That was the terminus of our conversation. I stood up, and still he said nothing, only sat there, shaking his head side to side. I was taken away, escorted by the guard he summoned with a button on his desk, feeling triumphant, but in a strange way, as if I had just been engaging in a one-sided conversation with the Mad Hatter.

After I was pronounced guilty at my trial, they led me back to my cell to await sentencing. Where I was raped by another inmate on the thirteenth day of my imprisonment.

Do you suppose my attacker to now be in the cell next to mine awaiting the same fate as I? No, he is not. I mentioned to my jailers at New Haven what had transpired, but to no avail. The general reaction was laughter and the follow-up was the comment that what "goes 'round, comes 'round" sort of theory, that I had gotten my just deserts as it were.

The rape itself was unimportant. I felt nothing during it other than wishing he'd speed it up. Oh, a brief thought flashed through my mind questioning my manhood for submitting, but I attributed that to childhood conditioning and passed it on. The man, a burly rustic with missing molars, threatened my life with a razor blade ingeniously fashioned into a weapon by melting a toothbrush handle and affixing the blade thusly to it, but I didn't submit out of fear for my life. Prolonging my existence by a few weeks or months by trading for passive submission seemed like a poor bargain, but the pain and agony of a slit throat seemed a poorer one, so I selected what to my mind was the lesser of two bad choices. Everything considered, it wasn't that terrible of an experience. I certainly don't know why people get upset about it and want to take people's lives for it and castrate them and boil them in oil and so on. As I say, I recall impatience as the chief emotion; I just wished to hell he'd hurry things along.

There was another feeling: Hatred. Not for the physical act of rape—that was no more significant than the rubbing together of elbows. No, what was despicable was that he was socially beneath me and performed an act upon my person without my permission. I would have felt an equal repugnance at his rushing up and grasping my hand with the intention of shaking it. If he had been above me in station, as I was to Miss Carlyle, the deed would have been innocuous, but he was decidedly inferior and therefore, his action unconscionable.

It hurt, certainly, but then so does a fishhook in the thumb, and of the two the former offers the lesser discomfort, and the fact remains that the memory fades as any tender feeling does, after ejaculation.

I tried to compare this experience to when I was the aggressor, but it doesn't translate. One was male to female, superior to inferior, and the other involved inferior to superior, male to male, making it akin to comparing the infamous apples and oranges.

I wish to waste no more time discussing this. In the

scheme of life, the incident matters very little. If you choose to view it as some sort of poetic or cosmic justice, then by all means do so, but leave me out of it, as I cannot subscribe to such an insane idea.

Such a philosophy reminds me of an incident in my teenaged years. A neighbor lad would go round and round the neighborhood shooting sparrows and other birds with his BB gun. Warnings from all the women on the block to the effect that someday he would "put somebody's eye out," failed utterly to deter him. One day, he was run over and smashed by a milk truck and these same women went about, clucking their tongues against the roofs of their mouths and saying in pious tones, "See? I said he would come to no good." As if one led to the other. As if their God sat in Heaven, looking down on his ant farm from His super roost and upon espying such behavior yanked the pipe out of His mouth and shouted, "Damn it, that damn kid shot another one of my sparrows! I'll fix him. I'll send a milk truck around to squash him!" What kind of philosophy is this? Deity by Loony Tunes? This is the kind of hysteria you get when society begins to believe in the gods it has created. After a time, God begins to take on the worst qualities of humanity and to raise them to exalted new heights.

Here comes Mr. Timex with my coffee. It should help me to get to sleep. My metabolism is such that stimulants work in the opposite fashion. Coffee renders me drowsy.

Now that was quite pleasant. For once, he didn't announce the infernal time. Probably forgot and when he realizes his omission will be back with his bulletin. And did you hear his words when he left? Always the same. "Have a nice day." Ugh.

This coffee is execrable. I never took sugar or cream before coming here, but this stuff needs a disguise. What I would give for some good chicory .

They brought a Catholic priest by last week to talk to me. What a boor. If I were stupid enough to belong to any religion, organized or no, that would be the last one I'd choose. All that bead twisting and mumbo-jumbo with the hands. I would think Catholicism to contribute greatly to the spread of arthritis. All that time on their knees, you know? Bad for the joints.

You didn't think me capable of a joke, did you?

The time has passed pleasurably here in my cell. I prefer solitude and this life suits me. There are a minimum of distractions; before today, Mr. Timex's visits were not as they are now, as the sands of the sea, and meals were brought to us, negating the need to visit the prison dining room, which they insist on calling a "chow hall" —I keep having a mental picture of rows of dogs sitting upright and eating Gravy Train from metal trays with Queen Anne silverware. Like Pythagoras , I eat no beans, so my diet is diminished, but then I have never required much in the way of sustenance, having a marvelously efficient machine, so there is no hardship there.

I read from the limited selection; currently, I am on the Russian, particularly, *The Possessed.* My choice was prompted partly by my circumstance and partly by my warder. You will think this odd, but my literary tastes are quite eclectic. I jump about from Balzac to, say, Goyen, without missing a beat. I keep my life ordered, my pleasures diverse, and thus have led a structured but exciting life, not without some element of spice in the sauce.

I am allowed a walk twice daily in clement weather, accompanied usually by Chuck, one of the guards, or "hacks" as they are referred to by the inmates. My promenade is always the same. Out of the cell, north along the corridor past three other empty cells, through the big double doors (barred, as are all doors and windows), past a smallish open-air alcove, opposite of which stands a small green door, through another big double door, toward an outside ramp that leads to an open-air concrete exercise area, walled on all sides, measuring fifteen feet by twenty-five. I am giving an estimate; I have stepped it off and calculated the footage, but this seems accurate. We are still four floors above the ground here, and my exercise yard is the flat roof of the administration building. There is one place, when we pass through the first double doors, where the walk juts out a foot or so that is open, guarded only by an iron rail that stands waist-high. On my first walk I strolled over and peered down the side; it plunged five stories to the ground and resembled looking down an elevator shaft, the edges of the surrounding buildings creating a seventy-five foot long rectangular tube. I got only a cursory glance at it, as the guard clutched my arm and hustled me away from it, not being familiar with my personality at the time and fear-ing a suicide attempt. The guards talk about that danger at times and all agree it should be boarded up, but theirs is a prison mentality, just as much as the inmates', and until someone higher up orders it done, it will remain as it is, I think.

That alcove holds another fascination for me. The green door that stands on my right as I pass the doors is where the gallows are housed, and I am permitted to peek through the tiny barred opening whenever I please, to view the interior. It is a simple room, roughly thirty by forty feet in diameter by my guess, and there are three gallows, their ropes suspended from the ceiling directly over a stage. The ropes, at present, are attached to sand-bags. I have already requested that my noose be the one to the left of center. My choice is a humorous one. The thief Christ forgave was to his right and I feel not that need. If I opt for the gallows over the firing squad (I am still vacillating between my options) I considered selecting the center gallows, but that would have given Lars grist for his attempts at psychological chess, so I will defer, although secretly, I have a preference for it if that is the way I must end. At the present time, I think I am leaning toward the gallows rather than the bullet.

Chuck, my guard at these times, is a likable, though simple man. He is mannered enough to call me "sir" and from time to time brings me treats his wife has baked. He knows I am fond of oven-baked bread, and his wife is an absolute genius at this sort of cookery. Somehow, he manages to get it to me while it is still warm, and the only obstacle to this delight being truly perfect is the absence of a cup of good chicory coffee.

One day, as we took our parade in the courtyard, the clouds opened up and a heavy rain erupted. This made Chuck nervous, as they are under orders to hasten us inside during such weather, the fear being we might catch pneumonia and thereby thwart the hangman (or riflemen). They are obsessive about this possibility. I pled with him to allow me the pleasures of the elements and he relented, even at the peril of losing his job should his superiors discover his laxity. This, however, endeared the man to me, and unbeknownst to him I have made him a codicil to my will, leaving him the princely sum of one hundred thousand dollars. The addendum is written in my own hand and secreted in my cell.

I was drenched in a second and it was marvelous. The temperature dropped to about forty-five degrees and was exhilarating. Even though Chuck had committed himself, and I could have remained out in the downpour for my allotted time, I took pity on him and volunteered to come in after only fifteen minutes. His relief was so visible and marked, I had to chuckle.

We went directly to the shower area where I stood under a scalding hot spray for a long time as Chuck looked on.

After, he did a thing that could easily have cost him his position. He walked me down to the prison dining room and got us both a cup of coffee and a Danish roll. The hall was deserted except for two or three convicts clad in white coveralls who were sweeping and mopping some distance from our table, cigarettes dangling from their lips.

"Truman," he said, ladling spoonfuls of sugar into his cup. "Why did you do it? I mean, you're not the usual kind of guy we get in here."

I smiled at his question. Like all innocents, he categorized people, and when someone happened along who didn't fit their box he was flustered.

"I was framed," I said, playing.

"Shoot!" he laughed. "I read your file."

"Okay," I countered, "what do you think, then?"

"I think," he started, and then paused, furrowing his brow into wavy lines, "that you're some kind of genius that doesn't belong anywhere. I'd say you're like movies I've seen sometimes where the main guy has been miscast. Like a comedy that isn't funny because the hero isn't. I mean, the lines are funny, you can see that, but you don't laugh because the actor doesn't say them right. It's like he's in a different movie than the others." He stopped again and took a deep breath, looking up obliquely at me. "That's you. You're in a different movie than the others."

I know I showed my amazement. I couldn't avoid it; he had caught me completely off balance. This simple prison guard had shown more depth of understanding, more sensitivity to the human condition, than all of the psychologists, behaviorists, and psychiatrists I'd encountered put together, with their framed degrees, lists of tomes read, conferences attended, and affected mannerisms of studying you over the tops of their glasses as they posed their insipid questions. In his straightforward way, he had cut through the subterfuge and claptrap and identified the truth. At that moment, I felt closer to that man than I had anyone at any point in my existence. It was then I decided to include him in my will.

"Tell me...Chuck," I said, when I had recovered a bit. "Do you have ambitions?"

"Not really," he replied. "I mean, I don't want to be President of the United States or be a movie star or anything like that." He stopped and thought a moment. "I would like to bowl 300 some day, though. I guess that's an ambition, isn't it?"

I granted that it was, and again felt a warmth for this man. His needs and wants were so simple and pure that he reminded me of myself in some ways. Don't get me wrong; he wasn't by any stretch of the imagination on my level, having not the breeding, knowledge, nor intellect I possess, but then, he didn't aspire beyond his station either, and it seems to me, the world would be an infinitely better planet were there more like Chuck breathing its air.

I would have requested Chuck be one of my escorts at my execution, but if events transpire the way I believe they will, everyone connected will undoubtedly be subject to punishment, possibly even discharged from their jobs, so I haven't asked for his presence.

Yes, I have a plan. To thwart my executioner.

This is it: I am going to fly from here tomorrow morning.

I have recaptured my old ability. For weeks now, I have been secretly practicing late at night when no one's about and all are sleeping. For a month, I've been able to leave my body and hover above it as I did as a child, and as soon as I regained that ability I began to attempt flight also. It was more difficult to achieve this time, as I didn't have the luxury of a hill to begin on, and for weeks I remained grounded, attempting, as I was, to levitate from a standing position. At last, it dawned on me that my lack of success lay in trying too hard, and I needed to go back to basics, i.e., clearing my mind, totally relaxing, and converting the cells in my body to weightless matter. Three days later I achieved flight. Not flight really, not that time, but levitation. I rose straight up above the floor of my cell for the grand distance of two inches. But what an achievement! I knew then that the initial distance wasn't what mattered; what mattered was that once again I could do it. To achieve my goal would only require more practice, and this is what I have been doing late at night. Practice, practice, practice! That is why you notice the black pouches beneath my eyes. They are not from the stress of my situation as my jailers would believe. I catnap as I can during the day and fly about my cell at night.

Yes, that's right. I can fly at will now. From a standing or even prone position. I am ready.

I see several questions half-formed in your mind. If

dying doesn't concern me, why escape? Ah, but I am not going to escape. Permanently, that is. I only wish to show them that I can. Once I am free, I shall fly back and carry out their sordid little drama. If living longer had been an ambition, I would have lied at the onset and escaped everything. They can't seem to understand that I don't care; this demonstration will exhibit that in a dramatic way. If I simply wished to escape, I would have done so yesterday or last week. I had the ability and opportunity.

Tomorrow, I fly. My execution is scheduled for precisely six-thirty a.m., and I shall soar into the heavens at precisely six-twenty-eight a.m. I can see their amazed faces already.

The guard has just wakened me with his flashlight for the two o'clock check. I hear him walking away, and then I hear the big double doors at the end of the tier open and then close. I have time for another practice session. I feel strong, sure of myself. I am so close to perfecting flight, I can sense the nearness of my goal.

I concentrate, slip into the part of my mind that allows this phenomena. My surroundings fade, fall back. I wash my mind clean, regulate my breathing. My body disappears and I . . .

Now we see in a mirror, in darkness, but later we shall see face to face. Now I know in part; but later I shall know as I am known.

—Cipriano de Valera, translating from St. Paul (I Corinthians, 13:12)

Chapter Two: The Past

...am floating; I am flying. High, high above the green-blue planet. I swoop down, low, and lo! there is a house. It is robin's egg blue and has white shutters and a white picket fence. Norman Rockwell put it here for my experience. I call it "experience" for it is not exactly a dream, not exactly something that is happening in real-time. It is an experience.

The house looks vaguely familiar. Ah, I see. No wonder. It is my house. The house I grew up in and have lived in all my life.

I go closer. It is not what I want to do; I want to clear out of here, fly somewhere—*anywhere*—else. Here it is bright and sunny and foreboding. I want peace and darkness. It is as if something were compelling me to draw closer.

I don't know how I am flying, the mechanics of it. I

can't see my arms or legs or any part of my body, and I just passed through a tree without sensation of any kind. I thought I could do it and I did. This must mean I'm formless, except that in all other things I feel as though I am contained in a body. It's strange.

I feel as though I should fight this force that leads me on, but the part of me that resists seems to float on ahead, or behind somewhere. It's attached but not directly, as if by some sort of silvery, wispy cord.

I'm in the house itself now. Things have a strange continuity—events are joined but spasmodically. I blink and I am in the next frame of the movie. Yes. This is my house. Or rather, this was my house. The things in it are my mother's. I had long ago thrown them out and replaced them with less odious articles. There is her worm-brown couch and the matching chair, two sodden lumps of shit dumped in the sitting room along with a hideous olive-green bean bag. I had forgotten how much I detested this room. The carpet is the same color as the insides of a caterpillar squashed on the sidewalk. It is impossible to paint an accurate picture of how awful this room looks. It is a nightmare.

What? There is my mother. This can't be. She's been dead twenty-four years...but there she is. I'd forgotten her features, but now I recognize her. Her face is monstrous.

She is rocking. In that chair, the color of offal. How I remember that chair!

There is something in her lap. She just leaned over

and kissed it. It's an infant! I feel ill. Faint and nauseous. A sense of dread washes over me. Where did she get a baby? I was the only child she had to the best of my knowledge. I am forced nearer. Can't she see me? I'm a yard away, a foot. If she looks up...

She looks up! She leans back in the chair and peers directly at me! What is this? There is no sparkle of recognition in her dull, brown eyes, no fleck of light. They stay the same. *It is I, Mother,* I fairly shout, but she has lost her hearing it seems. Her sight, too, must be failing. I could reach out and touch her I am so close.

My arms shake. I can't see them do so, but I feel them. My throat is seared with fire, and hot, salty perspiration collects and pours from my armpits and forehead. I quake, and my tongue cleaves to the roof of my mouth. I am agitated and sore, sore afraid.

I don't want to look at what she is clutching in her lap but, horrible, unseen force! my eyes are drawn to that swaddling lump. The blanket parts for a second and I see a face.

It is my own.

I gnash...my teeth...my eyes...roll...back into my head. I swoon...I want to swoon...but cannot...

My heart has stopped; I draw no breath; blackness is before and about me; I see only my mother and myself; I am here but I am *there* as well, held prisoner in that damnable chair. I cannot breathe. It is the blanket; it smothers me. Now I remember the smothering. Always the blanket she puts over my face. It is so dark; I am paralyzed in fear. I wet myself, and the smell of my own urine terrifies me; there is also the stink of my own shit. I am soiled and swimming in the stuff and always, above everything, I smell my mother and her odor of talcum powder and lavender and onions. She puts onions in everything. It is even in her breast milk.

Now I remember. It all comes back to me with a rush. The smell of onions did it for me. I can't abide the vegetable, cooked or raw, cold or hot. Her stink pervades the room. Onions. How can I smell and yet not see or feel my body? I am a spirit, right? A ghost?

So his is what it's like, being a ghost. The onion stink brings back my hate, and the hate brings back my courage. I float over to the brown chair and sit down. I sit more from habit than need; hovering over my mother isn't tiring. In fact, nothing that I've done so far is tiring. Do ghosts require sleep? I try a yawn as an experiment, but the result is inconclusive. I opened my mouth, at least it felt like I opened my mouth, but in truth, I couldn't tell for sure. There wasn't the feeling usually accompanying a yawn. I should find out later, I think. If I feel sleepy, then I'll know. This state has advantages I could see already. I needn't worry about where to lay my head. Never again would I need a bed or have to waste that third part of the day.

Another thought strikes me. Do I no longer require food? I go through the other exigencies speedily: pain, thirst, bowel movements. Am I truly free? Free of all the worrisome and nettling things that waste so much of our lives? Elation courses through me.

But wait. I am out of the body now, but seconds before I was in her lap and shitting myself. A memory. That's all it was, real as it may have seemed.

I have another thought. Where are the other ghosts? It isn't logical that I am alone. There must be billions upon trillions of us. But…I've encountered none. Even though my adventure has just begun I should have seen one or two by now. Unless…

Unless what? I have no answer. I look over at my mother, drooling and cooing over the lump in her lap. I recall her religious prattling. Of Heaven and Hell and Limbo. Is this Limbo? Where are the others? Surely, I would not be allowed to wander about by myself, but would be kept locked up in some great room somewhere with the other lost souls.

I laugh. Here I am, giving her superstitious twaddle credence! I have almost been fooled. It is obvious I am not a free spirit. I have been brought here by someone who has authority over me: someone with more power than I. Somehow, I am in a different world, but the rules are the same as the old one. There are hierarchies of power. I am obviously on a lower level. It is the same as the old world. One can never determine one's own fate; it is always in the hands of others. Well, they have miscalculated with me. It matters not a whit what they did with me in my former existence; it matters not a jot here. And if I leave this world for yet another at the end of your appointed stay then that one will perhaps be of a different form, but the structure will remain the same there too.

They seek to make me mad with this knowledge, I think, smiling. They don't know me. I'm not like the others. I knew this about the old world. I only thought it might be different in the next. So it is the same. What of it? I existed very well in the last, and I will exist very well in this one. And the next and the next.

I wonder what the crimes are in this world? Rape is probably impossible, as would be theft. Come to think of it, without a physical body as I have always known it, what crimes are even possible? Spying on my past? Detesting my mother? Perhaps there is no such thing as sin or crimes against others in this new existence. I wonder then, what is the key that unlocks the door to send you to the next form? I can't believe this is the end, that all who die are doomed to wander about for eternity, flitting about from here to there across time spans and geographical distances voyeuristically. Even if it starts out that way, as long as humans are more than one, they will begin to bargain, to plot, to plan, to scheme, to take advantage of, to recreate their reality. I cannot be the first in this hemisphere, and I cannot be the sole inhabitant.

I have an idea. The cosmos, the universe, is everything; it is all. We cannot even use a word like "universe" to describe it, as any word must necessarily limit it. It is indefinable. It is a cell that makes up a dog's toenail; the dog dies and the cell lies on the ground with all of his other toenail cellmates until a black, shiny beetle comes along and eats him. He goes into the stomach of the beetle until the beetle's enzymes and acids and juices change him into another form that goes to make up the beetle's antenna, and then the beetle crawls into a rotten piece of wood that the farmer's son finds and brings home to throw on the fire, and then he is burned and escapes from that world chemically into a piece of blackened soot that is borne up through the chimney into the night air and finally comes to rest on the neighbor's yard where in the spring he is turned over into the soil by the plow and absorbed into the young corn stalk, and so on and so on and so on.

That is only one tiny cell. Then, many of the cells go together to make up larger things, people, and trees and locomotives, and planets and novas and constellations and galaxies and universes, and on to the largest thing we can imagine, and the largest thing we can imagine is simply one cell that is part of something even larger, and so on and so on and so on.

And we are just like the individual cell. Who can say each of these cells does not think, does not imagine, does not create a world and an order just as we do, conversing with other cells and imagining the world he is presently in to be the center of the universe, inventing laws both physical and social to guide his existence. Seeing other cells die beside him and disappear or change form, he formulates the postulation that he is immortal and upon death will go to some sort of nirvana, the same nirvana he imagines his dead comrades to have disappeared to. And what if this goes on forever, on all levels, going from the smallest cell to the largesse we know as the cosmos, and there is no limit on either end. There cannot be a limit. It is a telescope. As we peer through the telescope the world becomes larger; if we were to travel through what we think of as space, the world we view would continually become larger and endless.

It would work inversely, too. Through the small end of the telescope. A hundred years ago we believed the cell to be the smallest unit in creation. Then atoms were "proven" to exist and we had a smaller unit. Tomorrow, we will create something we will call patongs, which will be the building blocks of atoms, and the day after, a man named Luther in Germany will discover something he will egotistically call luterites, which will be the building blocks of patongs, and on and on. Remember the philosophical debate of the tortoise and the hare? That the hare could never catch the tortoise because he always had to reach half the distance between them? It is an impossibility—a goal that can never be reached. Infinity.

The same is true in the physical universe. For there to be infinity on the large end of the telescope, there has to be infinity on the small end. The hare will never catch the tortoise so long as both are moving. All he can do is run forever, another concept that completes the definition of infinity and makes it complete in its incompleteness. There can never be an end, and therefore there can never be a beginning. It is all a loop forming a circle.

Within a circle. Within an infinite number of circles. And because infinity has no definition, by definition, in reality there are no circles either.

All this I worked out, years ago, in my first world, or at least the only world I have a present memory of, and I believe this to be true. All we are, all anything is, is a changing, swirling, mutating, moving, speeding, chameleoning, burgeoning, shrinking, expanding, standing, flowing, bursting, heating, gushing, freezing, living, and dying piece of something which is nothing. We have emotion—electrical impulses; we have memories—self-manufactured defenses against admitting futility; we have society with attendent mores—that is... This is where I have trouble. I can't figure out why we have any of this unless there truly is a God who gives us these things so that we may perform in a manner that suits some purpose and has created societal laws that are nothing more than subsets of laws of physics. I come to a perfect circle, but yet I do not believe there is such a God. There is just no reason for any of it. There is no reason for me. There is no reason for you. There is no reason for snow to be on top of a mountain instead of in a desert. There is no reason for anything at all. There is no reason for anything simply because reason was the one thing the Creator held back, as His joke. There is no place for reason in existence, and so we strain in futile agony trying to invent something that is uninventable. And if the Creator is perfect, then how could He create something imperfect without destroying His own concept of Himself? Therefore, there is no Creator. Everything is just part of a gloppy mass that just happens to be there and does things and changes form.

But we have what we term a mind, and because of that we cannot view our environment with naked eyes but must clothe our surroundings, physical and ethereal. And that is what is different between you and I; I do not choose to share your vision. I do not see death as you do; I do not choose to see society as you do; I am not willing to react to the stimuli as you do, because I have chosen different materials for my visions.

I am here now and do not have my familiar body nor surroundings. So I will do the logical thing: I will wait for things to happen to me, and if things do not happen to me then I will cease to exist, or maybe I will change form again, this time to one that does not possess a memory of what I have been or experienced, and the whole process will begin anew. Perhaps I am an atom and shall be split; perhaps that is how we regenerate over and over for eons and only remember one or two lifetimes. Perhaps I am pure thought and imagine everything. Perhaps God is a thought, a giant nothingness that is larger than any imaginable universe and smaller than any imaginable atom, and I am a brief electrical impulse in that thought and do what other impulses do—create a world.

I am God.

There. I am on a riverbank. I've discovered a trick. I have only to close my eyes and imagine something else and I am there. I am seated and hold a fishing rod in my hand. On the end of the fishing line is a fishing plug. We are connected, yet apart. I do nothing. The breeze blows, and the hot sun makes the leaves of the old oak tree waxier and heavier. The plug strains against the current, trying to escape the leash that holds it. I imagine a large carp looking at it, his powerful tail jockeying himself into position against the same current. He wants to bite the plug but is afraid to do so. The carp is myself.

Then,

There is my mother again, and this time the baby on her lap is not a baby but a small boy. He looks to be five or six, and she is holding his head with a firm grip, forcing him to suckle her breast. He keeps turning his head, but with her superior strength she puts it back, mashing her nipple into his mouth past clenched lips. I wonder why he doesn't eviscerate her nipple with his sturdy white teeth, but the thought must not occur to him. I think he will not think of doing that until it's too late, one day at the end of his teens, standing by her open grave, regretting.

Now I know where I am. I am in my practice session. I am in a cell on death row and I have less than four hours before my execution. I can choose now to go on practicing or end the session. It is so clear to me that I am loathe to give it up. Perhaps sessions like this are a more perfect reality; when one has control of them as I do this one, I think they are better. I decide to go on with this one.

I want to see my father. I don't remember him well

and haven't thought of him since he died, but having the power to go where I wish and see what I will has brought his face to mind again. I erase clean my thoughts and go where my dream will take me.

It works. There is my father. I want to try this new power. I think of the neighbor boy with his BB gun. I make him aim his weapon and ping! Out goes her eye. This is delicious. Another new power.

I am back to my father. I can go anywhere, do anything. I am from the planet Krypton.

He is seated at some sort of counter. The light is dim, but there seem to be others behind him and to each side. Tables—there are people sitting at tables and booths. At his counter, next to him, are even more people. They look odd, strange. What is it about them, their countenances? Surliness, that's it; they all appear surly. There, one laughed, but his lip curls even so.

It's a bar. It looks like Joe's Tavern. It is, but the barmaids are different. They aren't Beth and Jo, but they look much the same. It's their tits. Joe likes to hire barmaids with heavy yellow hair and large breasts.

My father stands up. He talks to a man who has come up to him and thrust his face in his. I can't hear the words, but it's evident both are angry. My father takes a step back and lets fly with his fist, and the other man stumbles back under the blow and falls, striking his head on a table. He lies on the floor, and blood rushes from his nose and ears. Some men grab my father, and he shoves them away. He is boiling. He steps back to the bar and downs his glass in a long gulp and gestures to Joe who refills his glass from a whiskey bottle. I can see the bottle. It's Jack Daniels. He drinks that glass too, in straight swallows, slams the glass down on the polished bar, reaches into his trouser pocket and withdraws some bills, which he throws onto the bar. The other man is still on the floor being tended by several others. My father barely glances at him as he turns and strides to the door of the tavern. The other men glance up at my father, and their look is the look of the dog whose master is cruel and who would like to bite him save for his fear. Their eyes shine with luminous white. He walks out, slams the door and is gone.

Curious, I follow, not bothering with the door but melting through the wall. I lost him in the gloaming. No—there he is, getting on a bicycle and starting to ride away, the front tire wobbling from side to side. I float along just behind him. I see he is headed home via the shortcut. I've gone this way many times. Everything looks familiar.

Just ahead on his path are three other people. I'm sober and so see them before my father does. He rides between them and they scatter, one falling to the ground. It's a girl. The other two are men. My father stops his bicycle. He seems to know them and they him. They all seem drunk. They talk. I'm too far away to hear the words, but there is laughter, gesturing, slaps on the backs. The girl kisses each of them. They all leave together in a group, walking into the wood close by the tavern, leaving my father's bicycle where he has dropped it. I seem to recognize the girl.

It's Greta Carlisle! No, that can't be. It must be a relative, her mother perhaps. The resemblance is marked. I follow, heart thumping. I couldn't leave now, no matter what. They stop just ahead of me. No one can see me, but something makes me take shelter behind a large oak tree.

The girl begins to strip off her clothes. Nude, she lies down and one of the men unbuttons his trousers. They are going to fuck her. I fly straight up, right through the dead branches of the tree I was under, toward the stars. I go this way, then that. I keep seeing the man unbutton his trousers. It's my father. I see him take out his penis, hold it in his hand like a weapon. It is so huge, enormous! I feel dizzy. I feel faint, confused. I fly here, there, above the wood, and all I can see is that engorged penis. It is everywhere I go, first in front of me, then behind, chasing me, pursuing me like a heat-seeking missile. I can't outwit it; I can't escape it. It follows me, its blind, red eye glaring, pulsing, throbbing, pursuing me whichever way I turn. It is there, everywhere. I want an ax, a sword, to destroy it, and then I have a sword in my hand, a great, heavy broadsword! All I did was think it! I start to swing it and then to stop and am unable to. The sword has a mind of its own; it is committed. I strain, use all my strength, but the arc is begun and I am helpless. It controls me. Slowly, ponderously, inevitably, my arms wield the awful blade in its arc, and nothing I do halts it. The edge meets the penis and slices through the organ, slowly, ponderously, inevitably. Blood spurts, and the soft red meat parts before the sharp steel. I can't stop it. I scream. I scream and scream and scream.

My eyes close and I try to faint but it's impossible and then I hear another scream that's not my own and my eyes fly open. It's my mother that's screaming and I'm in her arms and my mouth is around her nipple and I can taste the copper of blood. I've bitten her nipple nearly off with my tiny white teeth. I'm six years old and I have a body that is firm. I don't know how I know I'm six, but I know. I know, too, that this is the last time my mother will breast-feed me or rock me in that chair. I'm free. She screams again and this time succeeds in disengaging me from her torn breast. Blood runs and I smile and coo.

Foolish woman! If our parts had been reversed, I should have thrown her into the fireplace. Even in her pain she takes care not to drop me. Instead, she hurries me gently into the bedroom and lays me down in my crib. Yes, I still have a crib, with bars on the side, and I am in the first year of grade school. I have looked at bars every night for six years. I hate it. This will be my last night in this bed. I know this, too, but I can't say how it is I know it.

My mother hurries out into the other room, clutching her wounded breast like a fallen bird, in both hands. The blood seeps over her fingers, and I hum a happy tune with no words. I can speak, even read, but I coo like I'm six months old and not six years old. I am so pleased. If I had a tail I would wag it.

As soon as she leaves the room, I climb out of my crib. I'm adept at doing this, having done so hundreds of times. I go into the sitting room, and my mother is nowhere in sight.

The front door opens, and my father appears at the threshold, clothes in disarray and stinking of booze. I can smell him from where I stand beside the couch. He doesn't see me in his drunkenness. He bellows out my mother's name, and she answers him. She's in the bathroom. He staggers in that direction, and they talk, their voices muffled.

I'm shaking. I get down on my hands and knees behind the couch.

I feel bigger. My body is larger now, and I have different clothes on. How this happened, I'm not sure. It just happened. I'm nine years old.

My father emerges from the bathroom. He's shouting, and I hear my mother's sobs behind him. He commands me to appear, his voice ringing like a thousand spoons on a thousand tin plates in my head. I quiver like I am two hundred years old and hide my face in my dripping hands. He finds me, or his foot finds me, and he plays soccer.

Stop this experience, my mind says, but all I hear are my own screams and those of my mother. The only sounds my father makes as he goes about his work are short pants of breath and the muffled thump of his work boot as it booms against my ribs, the one sound punctuating the other.

I don't want to play any longer—I sob, and my face is smeared with snot and blood and effluvium, and he keeps kicking me with his boot. My heart is breaking; this is my father whom I adore, my *daddy*, and he is hurting me and I beg him to stop, my voice tear-sodden and reedy, a thin, piping wail, and yet he continues, kicking and kicking and kicking, and I start to scream, for he is killing me, and it is one long piercing sound that wells up from where I do not know; it comes not from me, but it does, from somewhere I do not know about, and my scream goes on and on, frozen in an eternity, and at the very apex something clicks and the pain is gone, even though he has not stopped; no, it has not gone, it is there but it feels good, welcome, and I feel my mouth begin a huge, huge, *huge* grin, and each blow from his foot feels better and sweeter and *blessed*, and now I'm a man and I have to kiss my father, but he is nowhere, he is gone, and I am in a cell on death row and awake and on fire with my blood turned to ice and wet and shaking and there is a frothing on my lips and chin.

I have a choice now. I can come up from my experience and be safe in my cell, or I can go back and see what else is there.

I'm falling. I let myself go. I'm at the stage where I can still end it, and I know it, but the strongest force within me is curiosity, and therefore I will go on with this experience. In a while I won't know I'm dreaming; it will all be real to me and no different than when I'm awake. When I'm in this state, half in and half out of the dream/experience, I don't know which is the true world. I think both are reality and that there are even more kinds of reality than these. Time is a loop of wire that is endless and yet the same; our past, present, and future are on the same strand of wire, as are the dimensions and senses we are aware of, with others we are ignorant of. I clear my head of all matter and junk; I see it as debris floating about as in a space ship. I open a porthole and it's all whisked away. The cabin of my mind gets empty and windy; nothing remains behind, and then I'm outside, no longer in my mind's spaceship or any kind of container, but there is a cloud all about me, shapeless and white and sere, like the emanations of dry ice, and then a caprice. I know by that it is in my power to go anywhere I might choose, but it isn't the part of my mind that I'm familiar with; it's the underworld of my mind, the subconscious, the part that has been with me always but a part I've never been aware of. Like a malignant tumor, it's been a part of me forever, knows me inside and out; it rules me, I think, but egocentrically I feel in control even though I know that to be ridiculous; I will continue to pretend.

The other way lies madness, I fear.

Ah, there is something. We come into view of it, my subconscious and I, like a great gray silent spaceship puling through the heavens.

It's a planet. Ours, I think. There's no proof of that, just a feeling I have. The planet is in turmoil. Oceans are aboil, mountains spew up black clouds and red liquid fire, the firmament cracks and spurts out steam and melted rock that runs like diarrhea, and the sky is midnight blue with but starlight to interrupt the void and outline the furious motion below. It is a birth or a death, but which I can't ascertain.

I see something else. I'm closer to the ground now, and all about me are people running as if for their lives, and suddenly something switches like part of another movie has been spliced onto the one we were in, and I'm on the ground and am alive and running with the others. I feel; I feel *everything.* There is physical pain, heat; I'm burned, showers of sparks rain on my head, my hair is singed, and I smell it. Things, hard things, fall on my head and back, and they hurt. I'm bleeding, and I'm terrified, but of what I don't know. I feel sorry, and it's not just for me but for someone else. The ache is for my children, but that's insane for I have no children, only I'm in a panic to try and find them, and I dare not think they are dead, and that is in the back of my mind while I strain to keep it with those other demons whose faces I can feel but not see.

There are objects that fly overhead, and I don't know what they are, but they have lights, spotlights, search-lights, and then I realize the objects are helicopters and they're trying to kill me and everyone else running with me. We run every which way, like rats in a dump, and I smell napalm and brimstone, and the acrid stench of gunpowder scorches my nostrils, and my throat is seared with the heat. I'm not afraid, I say to myself, but my body doesn't believe me and runs with the others. I look for a woman whom I'm in love with; my only thought is to find her and shelter her and save her from this destruction, and I look here, then there, as I run, for her, for my mother and father and for my children, and there is no one familiar anywhere around me, all are strangers, all with fear chiseled deep in their bulging eyes with blackened gore streaming down their faces. Everyone is wounded, cut. I see arms, legs, pieces of bodies, what I know is human meat, lying about everywhere on the ground, the charnel a forest of bodies and parts of bodies that have been cut down. I trip over bodies, step on flesh, and wade through puddles of blood that try to suck my feet into the ground. There is blood everywhere, and it is like a tide; it keeps rising and is to my knees. I slough through, my nose useless for breathing; I use my mouth and discover I am screaming, have been screaming, and my lungs ache; I feel smothered and on fire, and then when I think there can be no greater terror than what I have, I first hear, then see, a darkness that is blacker than the black all around me coming toward me from the north, and I don't know how I know it is from the north but I do; I know all kinds of things but know not how I came by the knowledge of them, and this new thing is the most horrible yet; it is like a cloud but more, a fierce wind too, poisonous and deadly; if it reaches me something terrible will happen, more terrible than anything, and I try to run, but I am in blood and it's to my waist and I can only move a little; the calves of my legs cramp with lack of oxygen and exhaustion; I am trapped and my heart is bursting; there is no air; I cannot breathe and the cloud gets closer, closer, closer, above me, atop me, around me, before me, and then it is on me and the others, and my throat strains and bursts with the explosion and pain of my voice as I scream and scream and scream; my eyes shut so tightly that my eyelids crack like porcelain in the fire, and my head is in a vise and my body too, and I am being crushed and have no breath and then . . . it just stops.

Like that.

I'm in a meadow and the sun is shining and I hear a bird. Then I see it: it's a seagull and it's flying above my head, a curlicue against a baby blanket of blue.

I hear a sound and I roll over. I've been lying on my back. I'm on a mountaintop and clouds are near to my head. I could touch them if I chose. I can tell this is not real; why else would a seagull be on a mountaintop, far from the sea? Across a few yards of alpine flowers, edelweiss, sits an old man, a very old man, at a small table of wrought iron painted white, upon which sits a chessboard all set up and ready for a match.

He looks up.

"Ah, so you are finally here."

I stare, say nothing. I've never seen this man before, but he looks vaguely familiar. I stand and stretch as if waking. I walk over to him. He waves his hand at the chair across from him, and I sit in it. The table with the chessboard is between us.

He has on a long white robe, and his hair and beard

are both also white and long. He is very wrinkled and has pink eyes. I have never even heard of pink eyes on a human before, but they look as though they belong and couldn't possibly be any other color. I wait for him to speak.

"Truman," he begins. It doesn't surprise me that he knows my name. "You've kept me waiting, you know." He seems to find this vastly amusing, a deep smile in his eyes.

"You are ready to play?" His hand indicates the chessboard.

"I don't care for the game."

His eyebrows lift in surprise.

"And I thought you were an intellectual. You don't play chess?"

This irritates me. "Do you suppose all intellectuals the same? If there would be a single definition, then it would be that we are not all the same."

This answer seems to please him. I blink and the chessboard is gone. In its place is another board with checkers on it. I lift my head and sniff.

"Not checkers either?" He shakes his head, sadly it seems, and poof! that game disappears also. Now a deck of cards is on the table.

I rise out of my chair. The cards are gone so quickly that, though I had my eye on the table, I didn't see them vanish. He waves his hand, directing me to sit again. I do so, out of curiosity more than obedience.

"So," he begins, "you don't like any of my games.

What then, do you propose we do with our time?"

"Why do anything?" I answer. "And how much time do we have, anyway?" I think for a moment and take a deep breath. "And who are you and where are we and what's going on?"

He looks at me, and I swear his eyebrows form a question mark.

"Why are you asking me? This is *your* life. I'm here for as long as you wish. It's totally up to you, you know."

This is illogical.

"Am I having a dream? I just had a dream, I think. I'm awake now." I look at him. "Aren't I?"

He shrugs his shoulders. "If you want to. Perhaps it's not your life. Perhaps it's my life. Or my dream."

We are both silent for a time. He speaks first.

"Whosoever's dream, or life, this is, don't you suppose we ought to do something? I understand you're a man of action. Can you be happy just sitting around? I know! I've got it!" He brightens like Euripides in discovery. "We can rape someone. Or cut off your father's penis! How does that sound?"

I can feel the blood rush to my face. "Who *are* you?" I stand up and face him, my hands making fists. He cowers in his chair, fear shrinking him so that he becomes half his size.

"You won't strike me will you? I meant no harm."

I sit down again. It is obvious the whole thing is a game. Again, I am at the mercy of whoever it is that runs this world or plane or sphere or whatever it is, just as I had been in every other world. The way to play it is to just sit back and see what happens next. I relax, and as soon as I do, the old man disappears. Not only that, but I find myself back in my mother's house again, and in her arms, suckling her breast. This grows exceedingly wearisome, I think. The next thing I know, I am standing by her graveside and remembering how much I abhorred being rocked and suckled by my mother, and wishing I had bitten her nipple off when I was a child. It is raw and cold, and the new earth on her grave is soft and runny, like chocolate pudding made with water instead of milk. Then, in a trice, I am an infant again, back in my mother's arms, rocking back and forth, and I do it again, just reach up and bite as hard as I can on her tough brown nipple.

There is a soft moment of nothingness, and there I am back on the mountain meadow, lying on my back. The same seagull sweeps over my head again. I don't wait this time but get up and stride over to where the old man is sitting at his table. There is no chessboard this time around. I seat myself, not waiting for an invitation.

"Talk to me," I say. "Tell me what this means. Am I in a movie that keeps getting run back?" He says nothing, just sits there, looking. I believe him to be wise, with his white hair and beard and all. I think: At least he must know something.

He doesn't say anything for a long time, and my patience flags.

"Can't you speak now? You were full of words the last time."

He just looks at me and smiles slightly. I speak again, growing more irritated.

"Am I supposed to figure this out on my own? Is that the game? If I guess correctly, will you tell me? Is that your role?" Again, nothing. It's maddening.

"Let me see if I can figure this out. The Eastern religions are right . . . right? To achieve karma, you keep going back until you do it right. Then you achieve nirvana. Is that the drill?"

He keeps staring. Something moves on the table and lo—there sits a chessboard. I stare at it for a long time. Then I reach down and move a pawn. As soon as I take my hand away the board vanishes. I look up. The old man is smiling.

"Thought you didn't play chess," he says.

My irritation mounts. "I don't play," I say. "I think it's a silly, facetious game and overrated as an intellectual pursuit. Furthermore, I don't buy that crap that it helps develop reasoning power or facilitates the learning of logic or discipline."

His pink eyes twinkle. That is, if eyes can twinkle. That's the only way I can describe the way they look.

"I quite agree, Truman. You think many things are stupid, don't you?"

"What kind of question is that? Any thinking person capable of reason discovers many things to be stupid. Or are you one of those blithering fools that mucks about smiling all day at every idiocy he encounters?"

His lips part in a broad smile that reveal broken and

yellowed teeth. Wherever he is from, dentistry isn't a very advanced science.

"You're going to hang in a few hours, aren't you?"

I am caught off stride by the directness of the question, inserted as it was, out of context.

"What if I am?" I challenge. "You think that bothers me?"

He just keeps that silly smile on his face.

"Well, I assure you, it matters not in the least. I suppose if it were you, you'd be sniveling up to some frayed priest, begging forgiveness for your sins and everyone else's and asking some effeminate God to get you out of this jam." I hear the sneer in my voice and feel it in my lips.

"I don't know," he says, that same smile still fixed on his lips. "I've never faced hanging. I've been threatened with other things, however, and those have bothered me a great deal. For instance, once I was cuckolded by a wife I loved dearly, and although I had promised her death should she ever be unfaithful, when it happened I found I loved her so much I couldn't kill her. I did punish her, however."

"Was she beautiful?" I ask and am immediately ashamed at the stupidity of my question. I quickly follow with, "Was it when you were as old as you are now or at a younger age?"

"I was the same age as I am now. Of course, it was many years ago. I seem to have always been the same age. Although I might have been older. Yes. That's it. I was older, then."

Double-talk. How could anyone be the same age many years ago as now? Or older? Is this person supposed to be God? I decide to ask him, up front.

"Do I look like God?" he answers.

I assure him I haven't the slightest idea what God looks like, except for some artist's interpretation that, except for the beard, didn't look much like him.

"I don't think I am," he says, "although part of me suggests that at time I am. There seems to be another part of me that I don't know about that I get glimpses of from time to time that suggest I might be. I don't know, but I don't not know, either. I don't worry about things like that, in any case."

For the first time, his smile seems to fade, just a bit.

"I do seem to be all memory," he goes on, his face a study and his smile a whisper of what it had been. "I remember it all. But differently." Now, I'm sure that I am the one looking puzzled.

"You see, *you* remember things sequentially. You did this, then you did that, then this thing happened. You can jump around and pick up links of the chain, but my memory doesn't operate that way. It's just one big ball of twine. Everything's in there. Even things that aren't in there yet are in there."

His smile has returned. The man is a raving lunatic. It is evident he's been on this mountaintop too long. Probably put there by his tribe or society or whatever, to keep him away from the children.

"I feel strongly about the number three," he is saying.

He keeps throwing out tangents to the conversation. It is very difficult to know where he is heading. "Ah, well," he sighs, dismissing his words with a wave of his fingers, "we aren't here to talk of me, but of you. What do you think will happen to you after they hang you?"

Now he is on ground I can respond to. "It's simple," I say. "I'll just go on to some other kind of ant farm. I think I've had a glimpse of it already. In some ways it's different from my present state—for example, there's no physical needs or desires, but in all the important aspects it's the same old show. Someone still controls the environment and me, and pushes me here and there as He sees fit. Doesn't show much imagination on His part, does it?" I am trying to goad him. If he is God that statement ought to elicit a heated response at the least. Maybe he'd blast me with a bolt of lightning.

Not so.

"And how do you see yourself responding to that situation?"

That's easy. "The same as always. I can't do anything about it, so whatever happens, happens. I'll just go my way and react to my surroundings, and someday I'll trigger something that will send me to yet another state. It just goes on and on until God, or whoever, gets tired of the game and makes me into a grain of sand or a speck of newsprint or whatever He chooses. I'm not involved with any of those decisions as far as I can see. My job is just to be another ant on the ant farm and amuse Him. If I was like the other ants and couldn't see His Plan, I'd be concerned about staying forever on the farm and serving His pleasure, but I know better. I'd just as soon be out of it altogether. Going through fourteen levels of ant farms doesn't interest me, but I have no choice. It's all one and the same."

"What about humanity? Aren't you concerned with your fellow humans?"

I look at him. Is he serious?

"My fellow humans? You mean those creatures whose only aim in existence is to gobble up more and more of our natural resources? Or feed their massive egos in the name of 'knowledge'? *That* humanity? You're joking, right?"

He looks away for a second and then back. His smile is still planted on his face.

"What about love?"

"Ha! That's the biggest fraud of all. You're talking about glands. Organisms controlled by glands. It's all too silly to waste time arguing about."

He sits silently for a moment and then says, "Logic appears all-important to you. What if your reasoning is all wet, and there is a Hell to contend with?"

He thinks he's tricked me, backed me into a corner, but I'm ready for him.

"I don't think Hell exists, old man. I think men created Hell to frighten other men. It's not logical. And, if there is a God, then He must be logical."

"Why do you say Hell isn't logical?"

"How could a perfect God create something imperfect? How could a pure God create sin? How could He even conceive of it? Has He no control? If He has no control then He isn't very powerful is He? And therefore, not to be feared."

I'm wasting my breath, but there is nothing else to do it seems, so I go on.

"On earth, we are taught by all religions that you have to be good and pure and suffer humility and debase yourself at His feet and reach the very depths of suffering before He affords His grace and thereby 'saves' you. What this proposes is that you go through Hell on earth to gain Heaven. Or you can make earth bearable and, in doing, gain Hell. Neither is logical. And I don't even want to get into the concept of Original Sin. That's a bad cartoon."

For the first time the old man looks sad. His smile has disappeared for the first time, and his hoary head looks whiter and older.

"Your words discourage me," he says. "Could it be that God has been misinterpreted by man?"

I laugh. "Well, if He was, don't you think it's His own fault? If He's capable of making mistakes in His designs then can He be God?"

Sober is the way I'd describe the old man's face at this point.

"I think, Truman, that your 'logic' has misguided you. I think that you will learn that. I hope you do. I don't think you would really be happy to be a grain of sand or a speck of newsprint. I think that what you really are is simply angry. And that is puzzling. No one has ever harmed you, to my knowledge."

"You think me one of those mindless organisms that spends their life reacting to stimuli? My mother hit me so I hit my wife and kids? My mother kissed me so I kiss my wife and kids? That kind of mindless moron? I am a piece of clay to be molded, my shape determined by other fingers? I have no mind, no powers of reason? You give man the same abilities as God? We can shape others as God supposedly shapes us? Does God give away His powers so easily? To such lumps as most men are? Not a very worthy recipient, but then He created us, didn't He?"

I set him straight. "What has been done to me or what has not been done to me has nothing to do with what I am." I am aware I am speaking in a loud tone, my voice rough and edged. "I'm an individual, a unique individual, and I have created myself. I have provided all the definitions in my life, set all the standards, all the behavior patterns, all the thought processes, and I am Me!" My voice rises to fill the universe, echoing, bouncing off the firmament. "I am not a 'product'; I am a Man , and I am not your piece of pottery clay. If you are God, you can overpower me, enslave me, use me in any way You will; direct me to go here, or there; You can kill me, You can prolong my life here, You can place obstacles in my path, You can remove them; You can do all of this and more but the one thing You cannot do, now or ever—You cannot control my mind or the way I choose to use it." I stop, short of breath and devoid, suddenly, of emotion. Surprise sweeps over me. I have talked to this old man as if he were God himself. And then I don't care. Maybe he is, maybe he isn't. It doesn't matter. It doesn't matter if he is God. It doesn't matter if he is only a crazy old man on a mountaintop. It doesn't matter if he is simply a dreamed-up apparition. The truth, my truth, isn't dependent upon anyone save myself.

He speaks.

"Why did you slay your father?"

"Go away," I say. "Why do you torment me? I didn't kill my father. I loved my father. I went to his funeral. It was lovely, beautiful. He was good to me. He called me his 'little soldier'. Why do you say such a thing?" His words are a lie. I don't understand his purpose. My fingers are damp and like icicles. I want to wake up. I have the power to wake up, I know I do, but I can't.

"Don't you remember?"

"Remember what?"

"You stabbed him with a butcher knife. You cut off his penis and stabbed him many, many times. While he lay sleeping beside your mother. He was naked and snoring. Your mother woke and saw you, and together you buried him in the back yard. Your mother told the authorities he had run off and that was that."

"I couldn't have done that," I say. What is he talking about? I loved my father. It was my mother I detested, all those wet kisses and the incessant rocking and cuddling. Confusion sweeps over me. I can feel the world spinning on its axis. My head is throbbing, and I feel dizzy, disoriented.

I look and the old man is gone. I am seated on my bunk, and I have prison denims on. I am wide awake. I look down at the left pocket of my shirt to see if my number is there. 49028. I mouth the numbers silently, forming each one with my lips. *Four. Nine. Oh. Two. Eight.* I am back. It's over. Just a dream. A dream of lies. My father died in a car crash when I was nine. It was my mother who was evil. All of that suffocating love. I hear the turnkey approach and know what he is going to say even before he reaches my cell. "Three o'clock, Pinter. You've got three and a half hours to go," and then he is gone, and I'm not sure he was really there.

I'm all right now. I'll call Mr. Timex back and have him fetch me a cup of that abominable coffee, and I'll be fine. I'm fine already. If that was God, I think He will be disappointed if He thinks my dream has changed me, made me contrite. Ho, ho. I'm no fictitious Ebenezer Scrooge to be frightened by a ghost in a dream.

Turnkey!

Here he comes, as if he were waiting around the corner like a faithful butler. Heartwarming, isn't it? Somewhat akin to vultures lying watch just off the dying cow, don't you think?

Turnkey, I'd like some coffee if you'd please and two aspirins if you'd be so kind. Thank you.

He is obliging to a fault. On the one hand it makes him likable, on the other, despicable. What is it about our species that causes us to dislike the toady who only seeks to please and admire the tyrant who only seeks to crush beneath his heel? It is the strength we don't possess that earns our respect, illogical beings that we are.

I'll drink my coffee and cure my headache and lie down to sleep away my final three and a half hours. I shall sleep like an old man dozing in the sun, dreamless and toothless. When it is time to waken, I will take flight, and the adrenaline that flows will be the same as now, no more, no less. My pulse will be steady.

He died in exile; like all men, he was given bad times in which to live.

—Borges, Buenos Aires, 23 December, 1946

Chapter Three: The Future

It is time. I hear their steps as they approach. When they offered eggs and bacon and toast and coffee earlier, I refused, wishing my body free of toxins, even though I craved the coffee especially. I had a laxative and purged myself thoroughly, even to the extent of blowing my nose and clearing my sinus passages until blood appeared on my handkerchief. I am pure in mind, body, and spirit, and am eager for this adventure. Won't their eyes bulge when away I go!

They are at my cell door now. There are four: two burly guards, my warder-psychologist Lars, and a priest. I am surprised at the priest, and irritated, but I say nothing. I must not become agitated. He mumbles his Latin hocus-pocus, hands clasped piously, rheumy eyes brimming with fluid, and I laugh in his face. He crosses himself and looks nonplused, as if he is used to this from the condemned. I wonder if I am his usual parish. My warder is the one to exhibit his feelings, as I knew he would.

"Now, I shall see you sweat."

I pay him no attention, just as I do the others. The two guards are twin condominiums. They should know better than fear a struggle from me, but I suppose it is policy. I shrug and leave my cell, a spring in my step. I'm eager, alive. The priest looks crushed. I suppose he expected me to fall upon my knees and beg for last rites or absolution or whatever Catholics do before being executed. I should have asked for a Jehovah's Witness. I could have made one of them feel welcome for once.

I am out of my cell now (goodbye, cell; facilis est descensus Averni). There is some Latin for you, priest! My guards flank me, Lars leads the way—confident man!—and my sad-sack priest wanders somewhere behind me, mumbling. I have forgotten him already. We progress to the great double-doors, Lars reaching for them, pulling them open toward us. Just beyond them and to my right is the green door where my rope awaits me (yes, that's what I've decided on). To my left, the alcove. I step through the double doors, take one stride, and then bend quickly to my shoe as if to retie it. There are no shoelaces allowed on death row, as there are no belts or any other instruments that may be used in suicide; my guards know this, but they are simple, and the information escapes them as I have bet it would. They reach for me when I bend, but when they see it's only my shoe I'm after they relax and straighten back up. I mutter, "Shoe's untied," bend, and at the same instant throw my body into the guard on my left, knocking him off-balance. In the same motion, I straighten and charge, like a linebacker coming off his two-point stance, and reach the retaining bar where I vault to the top, balancing for a long second as everyone looks at me in suspended silence. Their eyes are round; I have seen this, and I make my mind blank, clear the brain of all material . . . and let myself fall. I am free and in the air. I fall too fast; I am not floating. I panic and then right the panic. I force my mind back to the right state, and then I am aware of a slowing down of my rush. I am flying! I will settle softly to the ground, land on my feet, walk around the corner of the administration building to the exercise yard just in front of it, and take off from there into the air and over the thick gray walls. I will go quickly until I am out of range of their firearms; then I will come back, soaring lazily just out of range but still in sight, and then I will return to the front door of the administration building where I will land and calmly await them to recapture me and carry out my execution. They shall be forced to acknowledge that I really do not care what they do with me.

My plan works to perfection, just as I have imagined it. I settle softly on the concrete walk. A perfect landing! I crane my neck and look up. Above me, faces appear over the iron bar I have just left. There is Lars—he is first—then the priest and then my guards. They are all there. I wave to them. Their expressions don't change.

It is as if they don't see me. I follow their eyes. They're staring at something at my feet and paying me no attention. It doesn't matter. I feel a sense of urgency. Soon they will think to sound the alarm, send guards to nab me. I walk quickly out of their sight, around the administration building and out onto the recreation yard. There are inmates all around, yet they do not acknowledge me. It must be obvious I am a new face, but years of conditioning prevent them from showing surprise. I shrug and walk to the center of the yard. I look back. It's curious. There is still no sign of alarm. It's been at least three or four minutes since I flew down to the ground and walked out here.

Then, I know why. Flying has become old hat to me, a normal thing. But for my warder and the others it must have seemed a wondrous miracle, an astounding and amazing scene. They're in shock. I smile and begin my ascent. No one notices! I was standing next to a small group of prisoners when I lifted off the ground and they continued their conversation as though everything was the same. There is something puzzling here, but I don't have time to figure it out. I must be on my way out of here. Any second now, my warder and the others will regain their senses and sound the alarm, and I'll be nabbed.

There! I'm above the wall, a hundred, now two hundred feet in the air. I see a commotion by the administration building. Guards and inmates scurry around like frantic ants after a boot has trod on their hill. The alarm has been sounded! It must be, but still I hear no siren, no whistle. I take a chance and fly down lower to get a better look.

There is Lars! He's coming around the corner of the administration building, and behind him are the two guards and the priest. They're carrying something. The guards, that is. Lars leads them, and the priest takes up the rear. The priest is crossing himself and folding and unfolding his hands. They all appear agitated. Lars' face is red, and he seems beside himself with rage.

The guards are carrying a body! It's covered by a sheet, but there's no mistake that is what it covers. The guards lower their burden onto the grass and step back. I swoop lower. No one notices me in the excitement. The priest reaches over and draws back the sheet, exposing the head and shoulders and chest of a man. Blood is everywhere. He looks familiar. I fly closer, just above the body, twenty feet above the ground, forgetting my danger as my heart beats fast and my head swims. There is something about the man.

Oh, God! No, no, no! It cannot be; it is impossible; I am here; I see my body; I feel it; there is blood coursing through my veins; my lungs expand, my hands perspire, my breath comes in gasps. I am alive! I see all the proof I need. Look, here is my hand! I go down, settle on the grass. No one sees me. I am standing over the man. His prison number is exposed on his shirt, blood darkening it but still legible. I read it, the numbers paralyzing me. Four. Nine. Oh. Two. Eight. In white stitching.

I cannot stand this. I just want to go fishing again along my river. My whole existence has been structured, orderly. I have experienced more emotional peaks and valleys in the past several hours than in the whole of my life. It is too much. Would that I had never seen Greta Carlisle. My life was perfect before that tramp. I forget that I don't care what path my life takes, what road I'm forced down.

I can't stay here. I'll leave, fly away. At least I have that. I suppose I'm a ghost now, but it isn't like in my dream. I have a body; I can feel it, touch it, see it. No one else seems able to, though. This must be another plane that somehow coexists with my former one. I can see them, but they can't see me. But I have a solid body. I never expected that.

Wait. I just passed through a tree. I am solid, but all else is a mist, vaporous. This, then, is the true world. My other existence was the dream. My forty-four years fly out the window; they seem to have lasted but for a moment.

My discovery elates me. I fly over the ground, away from the prison. I go through trees, houses, hills. They are all ghost objects; I am the reality.

I come to a mountain and fly up. There are limits, it seems. It takes ten minutes to reach the top. I cannot just imagine I am at the top and appear there; I must physically fly there, and I have limits to my speed. I appear to also still be at the mercy of physical laws such as gravity, although not the same extent as before. So this plane involves space and time and dimensions. I wonder if there is a state absent of these constants. It seems there are constraints everywhere and, therefore, true freedom doesn't exist.

It's my meadow! There is no one here; the old man is gone. But there is his table and the two chairs. I dart over and sit in one. It is solid, real. I pinch my calf; it too is solid, real. I feel my weight on my buttocks, pressing me down to the chair. I have to think, figure out what all this means.

I examine my feelings, try to determine my state of mind. Everything is upside-down, not what I expected. I've found I couldn't fly as I thought. Oh sure, I am flying, but not in the body I thought I'd be in or the state I'd be in. I resent most the fact I was unable to show Lars and the others that I really didn't care that they were going to execute me. That grinds at me. That was the whole point of flying away: to come back once I'd achieved my freedom and give that freedom back. A life should stand for something, otherwise I would be one of those vegetables to whom life is merely a period of eating, drinking, sleeping, consuming, farting, fucking orgy of sensate pleasures, devoted to satisfying creature pleasures, and I am more than that. I am above that, always have been, and now, no one knows that. My life has been spent in vain.

I realize I have created a paradox. I claim on the one hand not to care what others think and on the other need their opinion to justify my existence. I've tried to escape this but I can't. I need others to define me. Therefore, I must care about others to show that I don't care. If I demonstrate my philosophy in a vacuum, I don't have a philosophy. This means I am the basest of slaves. I have to become a slave to gain my freedom. Therefore, freedom is unattainable.

My mind is swimming, and I must have a way out of this box. There is a way—I feel there is—I just can't find it yet. But I have a brain and, it appears, all the time in the world to use it. I'll find the solution to my dilemma, and when I do, I shall gain my freedom.

Just as this thought enters my head, I look up, and the old man is there sitting across from me. The table is bare; he has not brought his chessboard. He speaks first.

"Hello, Truman. Have we talked before?"

I stare at him, my mouth agape. Doesn't he remember? It was only yesterday. He answers his own question.

"I see by your face we have talked before. Of course. We must have. It's just that I have a problem. We are in the future here and things are not yet chronological here. There are no reference points for me. For you either, anymore. Let me explain," he says. He sees the consternation in my eyes.

"My memory encompasses all things. A sparrow doesn't fall to the earth that I do not note it. Even if it hasn't happened yet."

He must have noted my jaw muscle twitching.

"You see, Truman, your memory is like a piece of wire that goes in a straight line. It is circular, forming a loop, but you can't know that yet. In fact, you will never know that. It seems a straight line to you; you were born, you ate such and such a meal on Tuesday, you raped a girl, and so on, one foot after the other, so to speak. My vision is different. I see the inside of the circle your loop makes—it makes up one tiny atom in my vision, along with an infinite number of other atoms. And, like all atoms, yours is moving at great speeds all of the time, although you aren't aware of that—it seems slow and deliberate to you. At least it did. But now you are in the future, and you will begin to get a glimpse of what I am talking about."

I haven't the slightest idea of what he is talking about and say so. He sighs, sounding like my old mathematics professor trying to explain calculus to my freshman mind.

"I'm sorry, Truman. I'm not explaining this well at all, am I? Let me try again.

"We need a point of reference for you. What is the highest number you can comprehend? A million? A trillion? Let's use a trillion. A truly insignificant number, by the way. Well, there are a trillion times a trillion and more loops like yours running around in my awareness. Can you begin to see my problem?"

I don't, but I nod. If nothing else, the old man is interesting. He goes on and I sit there, a rocky glaze in my stare, I'm sure.

"Now, the past and even the present aren't much of a problem. Everything has happened or is happening and is connected. It's *linear.* There are some enormous numbers involved, and they're all interconnected, but basically it's a bookkeeping function to keep it all straight. A computer function, if you will. Now, the future—ah, the future! That's another ball of wax altogether. That's my problem. Yours too, as you will see."

He assuredly has my attention now.

"Understand, it's all there. There's nothing that hasn't already happened or that is yet to happen that isn't there. But the future, well, it's all one big ball of yarn, and sometimes I don't know where everything is until it unravels. There's just too much of it to keep track of. Don't get me wrong, I can tell you what's going to happen to individuals, yourself even, but it wouldn't be fair to tell you and not someone else who might want the same information. The rule is, no one may know the future.

"How I ever got into this mess I'll never know. I've made some mistakes. Nostradamus was one, but I learned my lesson there.

"Anyway, it's all set up. Each end of the ball of yarn will unfold the way I planned it, but I don't even try to remember how it goes. It goes on forever. And it started in the future. Now do you understand?"

I confess to a vague grasp of the situation, but that is a half-lie. What he says next brings me to the edge of my seat.

"Which brings me to you and your problem. You see, you're here because this is where you wanted to be."

Seeing my confusion, or maybe reading my mind, he tries to elucidate.

"Let's say you were a practicing Christian. By the way, that's my least favorite religion. All those hypocrites. If you had been, that would make it simple. For me as well as for you. Upon death you would go to Heaven or Hell, whichever one you had your heart set on. Everyone is allowed to create his own reality. All that is required to make your reality a reality is that others create it also.

"I don't tell people that, but I plant that knowledge in them. That's why others of your species run to and fro trying to convince others of their belief. To make it real."

It dawns on me. Somewhat.

"But you, you have created a problem. No one believes like you. Not enough, that is. Oh, there've been a few, but they're here, there, scattered, and they're all in the future. You're the first. Now you know why there are no ghosts in your afterlife. I recall you had that question in your dream.

"There are at present some four million possibilities in afterlife. Granted, the great majority are in one of seven or eight places or situations, but there are many more creations than these. Some of the worlds have only one or two inhabitants; indeed, most of the minor ones do. I'll tell you this: in the particular afterlife you've created, there will ultimately be eleven of you."

He says this as an aside, as if he is imparting a state secret, leaning forward like a coconspirator. He leans back in his chair and resumes his monologue.

"On to brass tacks. You see, you are in the future. The problem is your uniqueness. If, as I said before, you had been a Christian or a Muslim, or a Druid, there would be an established place to put you. These afterlives were so popular in their time they have attained an order and structure and pretty well run themselves. I could have put you into one of those, and things would have been fine. But you, you have to have the odd vision, in point of fact have invented a peculiar fate, and I do not have the inclination to map out your route. And there will be more and more of you. It will get to be a big logistics problem."

He sighs. For the first time he looks older than old.

"What I've been doing, in cases like yours, is throwing you, wily-nily, into that big ball of yarn. Oh," he hastens to amplify, "there is a plan for you, but it's random and fairly much up to you. I know what it is, or at least I would if I choose to take the time to remember it, but I don't. What I'm going to tell you next may be difficult to fathom, so pay close attention."

It is my turn to lean forward.

"When I said I threw you, wily-nily into your afterlife, I meant precisely that. For you, there is no more chronological order. Your piece of wire has not become a loop, and time has ceased to have any meaning. Not that it ever did.

"For instance, while we have been talking, it has been 2001 A.D., 45 B.C., 6 million B.C., and June 4, 1952, A.D. As well as four other dates. I have come and gone from you eight times you are unaware of. You think this to be one continuous time frame, but it hasn't been. I have spliced eight different pieces of your wire together for this indoctrination period. You will forgive this, but I am as busy as can be.

"Your problem, at least in your eyes, is one of 'non-resolvement.' You are unable to establish that it mattered not to you that they took your life. You thought to fly away, escape, and then come back and allow them to carry out your execution, thereby proving your point. Since you were unable to achieve this, you feel your life useless and pointless. Well, I am renowned for my forgiving nature, and therefore you will be allowed another chance. But, I warn you, it won't be easy."

I don't care for the tone of his voice or his last words. Foreboding is the adjective that springs to mind.

"The only way to achieve your goal is to live your life over and make a better decision when the time comes. For instance, before they come to question you, you could have a different escape route planned that you know works, a tunnel perhaps; you confess, and then, before they can grab you, you escape, only to return to turn yourself in and accept your punishment. That way, there'd be no mistake in anyone's mind that their actions don't matter.

"It's only a possible solution," he adds, quickly. "Doubtless, you'll be able to arrive at an even better one.

"However." He stops and my pulse rate rises. The bad news is coming, I know it.

"I cannot let you have your former life over. That piece of wire is used up. We'll have to find you a new one, similar in all respects. The one I have in mind occurs in five thousand years. Or is it six?" He scratches a small bald spot on top of his head. He must have seen the perplexity on my face, for he adds, "It's not as bad as you think. The period that has to pass will give you the time to make occur the afterlife you created—be a grain of sand, an asteroid, a cell in a grasshopper's wing, et cetera. It's all in the plan. You designed it, remember?"

He stops talking. At last. He stares at me as I contemplate what he's said. My head is abuzz, whirling.

Then, the crux of what he's said strikes me. I had spent my whole life under the belief that I didn't care what happened, but it had been a lie. I said I didn't care, but in reality I'd always thought that my philosophy gave me control over everything and everyone and, therefore, complete freedom. But it hadn't. I was more a slave than anyone. I was more at the mercy of others than anyone else in my universe. Because I didn't care. Those who cared did something about a situation they disliked. I had simply let things happen and taken the consequences, good or bad. Therefore, I had relinquished control and, in doing so, gave up any claim to freedom. I sit there in stunned silence wondering why I have never seen this before.

I gnash my teeth and taste salt at the water that streams down my cheeks. Frustration wells bitterly up. I moan, I shake, I cover my face with my hands. I weep, weep as I never have before in my whole life, from the depths of my bowels, great wrenching sobs that shake and tear at me, leave me shuddering and gasping for wind.

And then it is over. I am a different person. I feel the absence of all emotion as I remember what the old man has said. A second chance. I am to receive a second chance. That is it. That is my answer. I'll take that chance. I'll take the five or six thousand years in whatever form assigned me stoically and then...

I'll do it all the same. Screw the old man. He just wants me to help him out of his mess. I almost fell for his tricks.

I withdraw my hands and lift my head, my eyes bright and shining and new, my mouth opening to speak, and...

He is gone.

The old man is gone.

And I'm not on the mountaintop.

I'm in my cell again, on death row.

And six people are at my door.

Two guards, shaped like condominiums.

One priest, fumbling with crosses and bundles beneath his cassock.

My warder Lars, teeth in a smile.

The turnkey, Mr. Timex.

And one more, who must be the hangman. I am aware of the others as the turnkey begins to unlock the door, but I cannot take my eyes off of the hangman as I feel the blood freeze in my veins and my balls shrink up in their sack of fluid and the perspiration run like open wounds from my armpits down my sides. I recognize his pink eyes, his horrid smiling pink eyes, and when he speaks, the words are innocuous, but I have heard the voice many times before, always in a meadow before now.

"Hello, Truman," he says. "I'm your executioner. Are you ready?"

I say nothing, only stare. Then I nod my head and get up from my bunk. I smile, then chuckle a little, and then a little more. Soon I am laughing so hard that tears stream down my face. I roar with laughter, the sounds of my guffaws echoing throughout death row. Five of my company stare at me in wonderment; one just smiles calmly, saying nothing. It is he I address when I can catch my breath.

"You almost did it. You came this close." I hold up my forefinger and thumb. I stand. "Let's go. I'm ready."

We leave my cell in a body and all that is to be heard is the sound of laugher. Mine. Even before we get outside, I know what to expect. Rows and rows of people, lining the cobbled street, all hooting and jeering and laughing and spitting and hurling stones at me. I stumble and almost fall at the weight of the burden I suddenly find myself carrying. Blood streams down my forehead, into my eyes. At the end of our pilgrimage, I see the three trees. The ones on the left and the right are already occupied. Mine is to be the center oak, but I know that and I know that I have always known that. I turn and say to the old man the words I have rehearsed all my life.

"Father, why hast thou forsaken me?"

ACKNOWLEDGEMENTS

There isn't space nor time enough to acknowledge everyone who had a hand in helping me to the place where I could write this and get it published—I hope you know who you are and accept my gratitude. But there are a few who I want to single out. First is Cortright McMeel, who has championed this book from the beginning. Second is my publisher, Jon Bassoff, who isn't afraid to publish controversial work and who deserves credit for designing the best cover I've ever had on any of my books. I'd like to also give a shout-out to my copy editor, Alice Riley, who did a superlative job. Thank you each and every one. One other person who validated this book years ago and gave me the confidence to believe it could be publishable—Dr. Francois Camoin.

—Les Edgerton

CPSIA information can be obtained at www.ICGtesting.com
Printed in the USA
LVOW10s1328130913

352351LV00003B/68/P